The Elson Readers—Primer
A Teacher's Guide

Cynthia Keel Landen
M.A., Educational Leadership; B.A. Early Childhood and Elementary Education; Elementary Teacher/Babson Park Elementary School

Lorrie Driggers Phillips
M.A., Curriculum and Instruction; B.A., Early Childhood and Elementary Education; Elementary Teacher/Babson Park Elementary School

Lost Classics Book Company
Lake Wales, Florida

PUBLISHER'S NOTE

Recognizing the need to return to more traditional principles in education, Lost Classics Book Company is republishing forgotten late 19th and early 20th century literature and textbooks to aid parents in the education of their children.

The Elson Readers—Primer, which this volume is meant to accompany, has been assigned a reading level of 90L. More information concerning this reading level assessment may be attained by visiting www.lexile.com.

The Authors

Cynthia Keel Landen graduated with degrees in early childhood and elementary education from the University of Florida. She earned her master's degree in educational leadership at the University of South Florida. She is an elementary teacher with eighteen years of experience and is currently teaching fifth grade at Babson Park Elementary School in Babson Park, Florida.

Lorrie Driggers Phillips graduated from Florida Southern College with degrees in early childhood and elementary education. She received her master's degree in curriculum and instruction from the University of Southern Mississippi. She taught for thirteen years.

ISBN 978-1-890623-24-1
Designed to Accompany
The Elson Readers—Primer
ISBN 978-1-890623-14-2
Part of
The Elson Readers
Nine Volumes: *Primer* through *Book Eight*
ISBN 978-1-890623-23-4

On the Cover:
A Traditional Farmstead, 1956 (w/c on paper) by Stanley Anderson (1884-1966)
Harris Museum and Art Gallery, Preston, Lancashire, UK/© Courtesy of the artist's estate/ Bridgeman Art Library

Table of Contents

The Elson Readers—Primer
A Teacher's Guide

How to Use This Book

The students' *Primer* contains shortened versions of the selections found in this *Teacher's Guide*. It is recommended that the teacher or parent read these longer stories orally to the students before assigning the corresponding selections to the students. Hearing the longer story will help the students more readily understand what the shortened story is about and how the important words should be pronounced.

The *Elson Readers, Primer* is filled with delightful stories for your child to learn from and enjoy. The book is organized in themes, which are of high interest to children.

You could start collecting pictures, books, posters, cards, stuffed animals, puzzles, puppets, and other educational items. These items are to be used as learning tools to go with the stories in this book. The collection should include items related to the following themes. (These are in order with the book.)

Cats and kittens
Birds
Doves
Farm
Pigs
Rabbits
Squirrels
Owls
Windmills
Cold weather
Holidays—Thanksgiving, Christmas, Flag, Easter
Ponies

Preparing your child for reading and writing is a step-by-step process. Children need to move through several stages where successful experiences prevail. The following suggestions are ways for you to help move your child through these stages: keep a vocabulary journal in a notebook, provide daily opportunities for drawing and writing, and read to your child, or have them read independently daily. Keep in mind that if your child is not reading independently yet, your model of reading will promote this skill.

Lists of words will be provided for each story. We suggest that your child learn these words prior to reading the stories. One way of teaching the words is for you or your child to write one word at the top of a page in the vocabulary journal. Your child can then draw a picture that illustrates the word. As your child becomes more literate, he or she can use the new word in a sentence on the same page. Another method for learning and reviewing the vocabulary words is by using index cards. The words can go on one side of the card and the pictures on the other. These cards are great for reviewing all the words.

It is important to keep in mind that reading is more than just calling words on the page. True reading is when you read something and can understand what the author is trying to convey. You will find comprehension questions starting with "Bobbie and the Apples." The questions will be written in one of three formats. The formats include: *literal*, *implied*, and *creative*. *Literal* questions are answered right in the story. An example of a *literal* question is: What is the little girl's name? *Implied* questions are not literally written in the text. Clues and background knowledge are used to answer questions such as: What time of year is it in this story? Children will look at the pictures and see, for example, children wearing long sleeves and raking the yard and infer the time of the year is fall. *Creative* questions are where children can dream and be unique. This provides a great opportunity for children to tell, draw, or write about their creations. They may be asked to take the part of a main character and give their reaction to a story event, or they may be asked to come up with a new ending for the story. At this stage of development, students should only be expected to answer these questions orally. By doing the questions orally, the child is free to concentrate on his or her answer instead of laboring over the mechanics of writing.

Always have lined and unlined paper and many writing tools on hand for your child. Children need to have the fine motor skills exercised by having many opportunities to draw and write. A great way to work on writing is to have your child draw a picture. You can then dictate what the child wants to say about the picture.

Research shows that reading to your child is the best way to promote successful reading. For the greatest results, read to your child daily. Let your child pick the books or stories you read together. Beware that children grow fond of certain books and will want you to read them each time. What they are attracted to is the sense of familiarity with the story. This is a positive reaction on your child's part and something you bear with as the parent, always keeping in mind the benefit this is for your child.

A Note about This Guide

Teachers and students alike may notice a difference in punctuation, capitalization, and spelling between the prose and poetry sections in the reader. Rules for these matters have changed since the original reader's publication, and we have decided that in the prose sections it would be in the best interest of the student to update these items so they will learn these rules as practiced today. However, the stories remain completely unabridged. We have exercised constraint, and typical changes consist of, for example: commas used in place of semicolons when appropriate, lowercase treatment of words not personified, or hyphenated spelling of words being contracted to modern spellings. We have, however, followed the traditional editorial practice of not changing these items in works of poetry, leaving these matters to the prerogative of the poet.

We have used *The Chicago Manual of Style*, 14th Edition, published by the University of Chicago, as our primary reference for these changes.

Objectives—

By completing the *Primer* the following objectives will be met:

1. The student will predict what a story is about based on its title and illustrations.
2. The student will identify words and construct meaning from text, illustrations, use of phonics, and context clues.
3. The student will use knowledge of developmental-level vocabulary in reading.
4. The student will increase comprehension by retelling and discussing what was read.
5. The student will determine the main idea and supporting details from text.
6. The student will use simple reference materials to obtain information.
7. The student will show an awareness of a beginning, middle, and end in passages.
8. The student will follow simple sets of instructions for simple tasks, using logical sequencing of steps.
9. The student will listen for a variety of purposes, including curiosity, pleasure, getting directions, performing tasks, solving problems, and following rules.
10. The student will retell details of information heard, including sequence of events.
11. The student will determine the main idea through illustrations.
12. The student will recognize basic patterns in and functions of language.
13. The student will understand that word choice can shape ideas, feelings, and actions.
14. The student will identify and use repetition, rhyme, and rhythm in oral and written text.
15. The student will identify the story elements of setting, plot, character, problem, and solution.

The Cat's Dinner, p. 9

One morning my big kitty, with her three little kittens, sat by the porch. We call her "Black Kitty," but she has some white spots on her thick, warm coat. Just then my sister Alice and I saw her. "See the kittens," said Alice. "They look hungry. Let's take them into the house and give them some milk. Come, cat, come! Come, kittens, come!"

But Black Kitty said, "Mew, mew. No thank you, little girl. We do not need milk today. This is hunting day, and I am going to teach my kittens to hunt for their dinner."

So Black Kitty led her three little kittens down the road until they came to a big orchard where they could hunt for something to eat. A plump little bird would make a nice dinner. And, sure enough, there was one sitting on a branch of the great old apple tree by the well. Black Kitty saw the bird, and the little kittens saw it, too. Black Kitty twisted her ears and straightened out her back and looked right at the little bird, as she thought of the fine dinner it would make. But the bird saw Black Kitty; it saw the kittens, too. Away it flew, and all the leaves in the orchard rustled together, whispering, "Nothing here for Black Kitty, nothing here for little kittens."

Then Black Kitty said, "Come, kittens! We must hunt somewhere else for our dinner. Come to the barn." So they went to the barn, for Black Kitty thought that she could find a mouse there for dinner. Black Kitty sat down near a dark hole in the wall. She sat there so long that she hardly knew whether she was awake or asleep, listening, listening, listening. The three little kittens sat still, too, listening, listening, listening. They wanted to learn how to hunt for their dinner. At last Black Kitty saw a little mouse come creeping and peeping along. Black Kitty crouched down very low and waited for the mouse to come a little nearer. But the mouse saw Black Kitty and ran back into the hole before she could catch her. And Black Kitty heard the soft breeze that came through the barn window, sighing over and over, "Nothing here for you-o-o; nothing here for you-o-o."

"Mew, mew, Mother," said the kittens. "Where can we go now to hunt for our dinner?"

But Black Kitty said, "We will not hunt anymore today. This isn't a good hunting day, after all. We will go to the house and ask the children for milk." So Black Kitty went to the house. The kittens went, too. When we saw them coming Alice said, "Come, cat, come! Come, kittens, come! Something here for you!" Then we gave them a big pan full of milk for dinner. And as they lapped up the milk with their little red tongues, the three kittens said, "Mew, mew, Mother! The house is the best place to hunt in."

—Lillian M. Allen in *Story-Telling Time*

The Cat's Dinner

Preteach the following vocabulary: cat, barn, bird, dinner, house, mouse, and kittens.

After reading the story with your child, encourage looking for the vocabulary words in the text. Use the journal or cards to reinforce this search.

The phonics lesson will review beginning consonant sounds. Use the vocabulary words from the story and chart other words that begin the same way.

This is a circle story because the story begins and ends in the same way. Have your child sequence the sentences on the worksheet. This is one format that allows the student to practice the skill of sequencing, which is one of the reading comprehension skills.

Answers to the sequencing worksheet

1. Alice said, "Come cat, come to dinner."
2. The cat and kittens saw a bird. The bird flew away.
3. The cat and kittens went to the barn and saw a mouse. The mouse ran away.
4. The cat and kittens went back to the house and had milk for dinner.

NAME______________________________ CLASS__________ DATE_______

THE CAT'S DINNER, P. 9

Sequence the following story events. Cut the boxes apart and glue them in the correct order.

1.

2.

3.

4.

The cat and kittens went to the barn and saw a mouse. The mouse ran away.

The cat and kittens went back to the house and had milk for dinner.

The cat and kittens saw a bird. The bird flew away.

Alice said, "Come cat, come to dinner."

Spot's Kittens, p. 13

Would you like to hear about my cat, Spot? She is a beautiful cat, with blue eyes and a black coat spotted with white. That is why we call her Spot. When we want her to come to her dinner we say, "Come, Spot, come." I like Spot, and Spot likes me.

Spot has four kittens. One kitten is white, one kitten is black, one kitten is gray, and one kitten is like Spot—black and white. Spot used to keep her kittens on a carpet bed under the kitchen doorstep. When Spot chose this place, she thought it would be a safe and comfortable home for her little ones. Here the little white kitten, and the little black kitten, and the little gray kitten, and the little black and white kitten ran and played and had all the fun they could want.

But one day the rain came. Down poured the water through a crack between the doorstep and the house, and poor Spot found that she and her babies were getting wet. "Mew, mew!" she cried. "We are wet! We are wet!" As we sat in the house we heard Spot mewing in a very loud voice just outside the kitchen door. Spot and her little family were trying to get in out of the cold rain. We opened the door in a hurry and took Spot into the house. We took the kittens, too. We put them on a mat by the kitchen stove. Before long the heat of the fire had dried their fur, and they all went to sleep. After the storm was over we made another bed for them in a place where the rain could not come, and Spot had no more trouble in bringing up her family.

—Josephine Jarvis in *In the Child's World*

Spot's Kittens

Preteach the following vocabulary: black, gray, white, and sleep.

Review previous vocabulary not mastered by your child.

Phonics skills will include introducing the long *e* sound and the *gr* consonant cluster. Introduce the long *e* sound by rereading the story and having the child listen for the three long *e* words: me, we, sleep. Then brainstorm more words with this sound. Circle the letter or letters that make the long *e* sound.

Write the word *gray* and have your child think of other words that begin with the same consonant cluster. Your child can then illustrate four words of his or her choice.

Answer the following cause/effect questions after reading the story.

Why were the cat and kittens wet? They got wet in the rain.

Why did the cat go to the girl? The girl called for the cat.

Why did Spot and the kittens go in the house? Spot and the kittens needed to get out of the rain.

Color the cat and four kitten drawings according to the story's written descriptions.

Answers

Cat—colored black and white

Kittens—1 white, 1 black, 1 gray, and 1 black and white

Note: The coloring doesn't have to match the picture exactly. Allow some creativity.

NAME______________________________CLASS__________DATE______

SPOT'S KITTENS, P. 13

Reread the story. Color the cat and kittens the way they were described in the story.

ALICE AND HER KITTEN, P. 16

One day when Alice was a very little girl, her father came home early from the office. He carried a basket in his hand, but when he saw Alice he put the basket behind him. His eyes twinkled with fun, for he knew that Alice would wonder what was in the basket.

Alice jumped up from her chair and ran to her father. Her eyes grew big and bright as she peeped at the basket that her father had put upon the floor.

"What is in the basket?" asked Alice.

"Can you guess?" her father said.

"Is it a bird?" asked the little girl.

Her father laughed. "No, it is not a bird," he said.

"Oh, I know! It is a little dog!" cried Alice.

But her father only shook his head and said, "No, it is not a dog."

"Is it a kitten?" she asked.

"Yes, it is a kitten," he answered. "You guessed right at last."

"Is the kitten for me, Father?" asked Alice.

"Yes, it is for you," said her father. "Just listen a moment." He held the basket close to her.

Soon she heard a faint, "Mew, mew," and then a little black head pushed up the cover.

"Oh, isn't she black!" cried the little girl. "I wonder if she is hungry. May I feed her, Mother?" Alice's mother gave her some milk, and Alice gave it to the little kitten.

The kitten lapped the milk with her little red tongue, until there was not a drop left in the saucer. Then she put her head between her paws and soon was fast asleep.

—Jane L. Hoxie in *Kindergarten Story Book*

Alice and Her Kitten

Preteach and review vocabulary: basket and milk.

This story contains repetition with the short *i* words: is, it and in. To reinforce the sound of short *i*, use the building words worksheet to discover familiar words with the short *i* sound.

Have your child cut out the consonant letters and try each consonant in the boxes to see if they form new words. When your child builds a word, have him or her use it orally in a sentence.

You may want to put this activity in an envelope or baggie to save for review. For an extension to the story, play a guessing game using words to describe something in the room or something concealed in a bag. Take turns with your child guessing the objects.

NAME________________________________CLASS__________DATE______

ALICE AND HER KITTEN, P. 16

Cut out the consonants and consonant clusters at the bottom of the page and place them in the boxes to make new words. (Do not glue the letters down.) Use the spaces provided below to list the words you have made.

☐it

☐in

☐is

b	f	h	k	l	n	p	s
t	w	z	sp	sl	th	ch	

What Was in the Nest?, p. 19

I will tell you a story of two little girls named Nellie and Katie, who lived away out in the country. They lived with their mother and father in a little house among the trees, where they could hear the birds sing and watch all the pretty wildflowers blossom through the spring and summer. In the autumn they would pick the fruit and watch for Jack Frost to open the chestnut burrs and let the nuts drop to the ground for the little boys and girls or the squirrels. But what I want to tell you about is something the girls saw one morning in June.

Two little birds had come from down south and built a nest in the cherry tree in front of the house. Now, the room where Nellie and Katie slept had a window that looked right out upon the branches of this cherry tree, and how the girls did enjoy watching the birds! The mother bird sat on the nest day after day. One morning she flew away for a few moments, and what do you suppose the little girls saw? They saw one, two, three, four pretty blue eggs in the nest.

The mother bird flew back to the nest and sat there day after day for two long weeks. One day she flew from the nest. She sat in the tree and sang and sang. The father bird sang, too. The little girls looked in the nest. Can you guess what they saw? They saw four funny little baby birds without any feathers!

The little birds grew and grew until by and by they were covered with feathers, and they were so large that there was hardly room for them all in the nest. When it was time to teach them to fly, the mother bird said, "Fly, fly!" The father bird, too, said, "Fly, fly!" The girls watched the four little birds learn to fly. They flew from the nest; soon they flew from tree to tree. One day all the birds flew far away, and the little girls waved their hands and said, "Good-bye, good-bye!"

—*Boston Collection of Kindergarten Stories*

WHAT WAS IN THE NEST?

Preteach and review vocabulary: nest, fly, tree and eggs.

After reading the title and studying the illustrations, have your child make a prediction of what might be found in the nest. Check the prediction after reading the story.

The phonics skills are introducing the consonant cluster *tr* and the inflectional ending *ed*. Have your child look through a magazine or newspaper to find pictures of things that start with *tr*.

Cut the pictures out, glue them to construction paper and label them with parent's help.

To better understand sequencing, have your child illustrate something he or she can remember from the beginning, middle, and end of the story.

Answers
beginning—seeing the bird nest,
middle—four blue eggs, baby birds hatched,
end—birds flew away.

For *ed* practice, use the provided worksheet.

Answers to the *ed* worksheet:

1. milk
2. walked
3. play
4. laughed
5. talked
6. look
7. warm
8. jump
9. wanted
10. rained

NAME______________________________CLASS__________DATE______

WHAT WAS IN THE NEST?, P. 19

Read the sentences. Choose the correct word and write it on the line.

1. I will go to the farm and _______________ the cow.
   milk   milked

2. My mother _______________ four miles yesterday.
   walk   walked

3. May I _______________ with my friend?
   play   played

4. The little girl _______________ when she saw the kitten run.
   laugh   laughed

5. The boy _______________ to his Grandma last week.
   talk   talked

6. _______________ in the basket for the eggs.
   Look   Looked

7. Mother said she would _______________ the soup on the stove.
   warm   warmed

8. If you _______________ in the mud puddle, you will get wet.
   jump   jumped

9. The baby cried because he _______________ his mother.
   want   wanted

10. I could not play outside yesterday because it _______________.
    rain   rained

The White Dove, p. 23

Once a beautiful white dove was flying high in the air. She said to herself, "The greatest fun in all the world is to fly and fly and fly. I am sorry for those who have no wings and cannot fly. I wonder if they are ever happy. I will ask the cow and find out." So she flew to Farmer Brown's barn and said to the white cow, "Coo, coo! See my pretty wings! Don't you wish you had wings? You could fly and fly and fly."

"Moo, moo!" said the cow. "Oh, no! I give milk to boys and girls. Moo, moo! I don't want to fly!"

Away flew the dove to the sheep. It said, "Coo, coo! Don't you wish you had wings? You could fly and fly and fly."

"Baa, baa!" said the sheep. "I give wool to boys and girls to keep them warm. The warm coats they wear are made of my wool. Baa, baa! I don't want to fly!"

Away flew the dove to the horse. It said, "Coo, coo! Don't you wish you had wings? You could fly and fly and fly."

"No, no," said the horse, with a toss of his head. "I give rides to boys and girls. No, no! I don't want to fly."

Away flew the dove to the hen. It said, "Coo, coo! Don't you wish you could fly away? You cannot fly away with your wings. Don't you wish you had wings like mine?"

"Cluck, cluck!" said the hen. "I give eggs to boys and girls. I don't want to fly away."

Then the dove called the cow and the sheep and the horse and the hen all together.

"Coo, coo!" she said. "Are you all happy?"

The cow said, "Moo, moo! Yes, yes!"

The sheep said, "Baa, baa! Yes, yes!"

The hen said, "Cluck, cluck! Yes, yes!"

The horse said, "Yes, yes!"

The dove said,

"Coo, coo, coo!
I am happy, too."

Away she flew to her nest.

—Harriet Warren

The White Dove

Preteach and review vocabulary: dove, sheep, wool, horse, hen, cow, wings, happy, and rides.

This selection has onomatopoeia words such as: coo, moo, baa and cluck. These are words that say the sounds they make. After reading the story, list this type of words from the story. Add any other words that belong in this group, like crash and bang.

For the phonics lessons, introduce the *oo* sound found in moo and coo. You and your child can then brainstorm other words with this sound, such as: ooze, pool, and too.

For the worksheet find words from the story to place in the chart under the headings for short *i* and long *i*. To extend this activity, you can name other words with these vowel sounds and have your child classify the word in the correct column on the chart.

Extension—select an animal and tell what goods or services they provide. Cut and paste animals under the headings "Goods" and "Services."

Answers:
Short *i* words are: wings, it, wish, give, and milk.
Long *i* words are: white and fly.

Note the spelling differences with the use of *y*.

NAME________________________________CLASS__________DATE______

THE WHITE DOVE, P. 23

Reread the story and place words with *i* vowel sounds into the correct column.

Short *i*	**Long *i***

The Jay and the Dove, p. 28

There is no long version of this selection. Instead, read the story orally and have the students memorize the entire story on pages 28 and 29.

The Jay and the Dove

Preteach and review the following vocabulary: jay, dove, and above.

This story is in the format of a play. Bring to your child's attention that a play is presented differently than a story. Point out that you can tell which character is speaking by the name in front of each speaking part.

Introduce the vowel sound of long *a* spelled *ay*. Have your child find words from the story that follow this pattern then brainstorm more words.

After reading the story, pick out sets of rhyming words: jay, play, away, dove, love, above.

Teach your child that rhyming words have the same vowel and ending sounds. To practice rhyming words, use the provided worksheet.

Extension, Creative Writing/Drawing—Write and/or illustrate what Mr. Jay would do in the land of play or what Mrs. Dove would do in the land of love.

Answers:
house—mouse
snake—rake
boat—coat
tree—bee

NAME________________________________CLASS__________DATE_______

THE JAY AND THE DOVE, P. 28

Match the pictures in the left column to the rhyming picture in the right column.

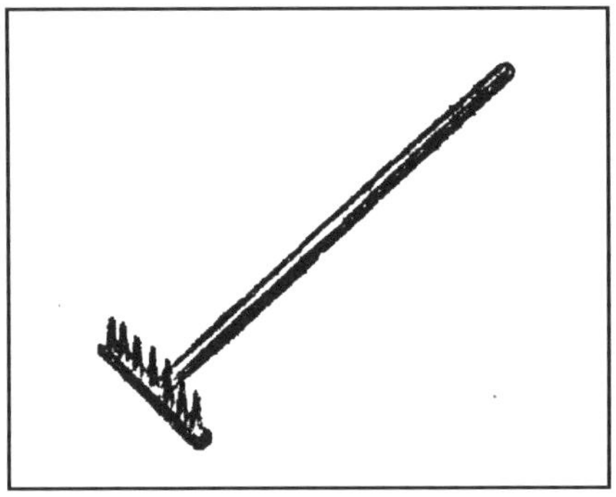

Bobbie and the Apples, p. 30

One day Bobbie's mother sat by the fire while Bobbie lay on the rug, looking at a picturc book.

"Ho, ho," yawned Mother. "I like apples. I wish I had some. I would show you how to roast them."

"I'll get some for you," Bobbie said, and he jumped up, put on his hat, and ran down the road to a big apple tree. He looked and looked, but could not see an apple.

"Oh," cried Bobbie, "where have all the apples gone?" And then he heard the tree say,

"I have no apples for you today.
I gave all my apples away."

So Bobbie turned away and started home across the field. Pretty soon he met a cat. "Oh, Pussy," he cried, "do you know where I can get some apples? I want some for Mother."

Pussy looked up at him and said,

"Mew, mew, mew!
I have no apples for you.
I want milk for dinner."

So Bobbie went on, and at last he met a friendly doggie. The dog wagged his tail, and Bobbie said to him, "Oh, Doggie, do you know where I can find some apples? I want some for Mother."

The dog kept on wagging his tail and barked,

"Bow-wow, bow-wow!
Go to the cow.
The cow will tell you."

"Thank you, Dog," said Bobbie.

So the little boy went on until he came to a kind old cow, that stood looking over the fence.

"Oh, Cow," said Bobbie, "do you know where I can find some apples? I want some for Mother."

But the cow said,

"Moo, moo, moo!
I like apples, too.
Go to the farmer.
He has some apples."

So Bobbie said, "Thank you," and ran up the hill to the farmer's house as fast as he could go.

When the farmer saw Bobbie, he said, "Good morning, little boy. What can I do for you today?"

Bobbie said, "I want some apples for Mother. Have you some?"

The farmer laughed. "Come with me," he said, "and I will give you some apples."

So Bobbie and the farmer went into the house and down into the cellar, and there Bobbie saw a bag full of big red apples!

"Oh, what a lot!" said Bobbie. "Why did you pick them all?"

"I did not want Jack Frost to find them," said the farmer.

"Does he like apples?" asked Bobbie.

"He just likes to pinch them," said the farmer, "but we like to eat them, so we gather them in for the winter."

"May I have three of them?" asked Bobbie. I want them for my mother."

"Yes, little boy," said the farmer. "You may have four apples. One apple is for you."

"Thank you, Mr. Farmer, for these nice big red apples," said Bobbie; "I will give three to Mother." And then he ran home to give the apples to his mother.

"See, Mother," he said; "see what I have!"

"Where did you find them?" asked Mother.

"Oh," said Bobbie, "I went to the apple tree, but it didn't have any. Then I asked the cat where the big red apples were, and she didn't know; and then I asked the dog, but he didn't know; and then I asked the cow, and she told me to go to the farmer. Then I ran to the farmer, and he gave them to me. Three are for you and one is for me."

"You are a good boy!" said Mother, when Bobbie stopped—out of breath.

—Kate Whiting Patch in *For the Children's Hour*—Adapted

Bobbie and the Apples

Preteach and review the following vocabulary: apples, morning, bag, and farmer.

This is the first story that will have comprehension questions. Refer to the "Objectives" for the different types of questions your child will be asked to answer.

Comprehension questions are for the student to answer orally. The student should look back at the text only when unable to answer the question.

Literal

1.Why didn't the tree have any apples? The tree gave them all away.

2. What did the cat want for dinner? The cat wanted milk.

Implied

3. What was the farmer doing when Bobbie found him? The farmer was working or walking in the field.

4. What is the story mainly about? Bobbie was looking for apples for his mother.

Creative

5. What do you think Mother plans to do with the apples? Accept any reasonable answer.

For phonics, introduce the short *e* sound by using the words *yes, get,* and *tell*. Extend this skill by having your child look around your house to find objects with the short *e* sound. As the child identifies objects, the parent can make a running list of the words.

This is another circle story, which will give your child more practice with sequencing. The student should cut out the words and glue them in sequential order on the worksheet. The student can retell the story while working or after the circle story project is completed.

Answers:
1. mother
2. tree
3. cat
4. dog
5. cow
6. farmer

Name______________________________ Class__________ Date______

Bobbie and the Apples, p. 30

Cut the words from the bottom to sequence in the circle story frame.

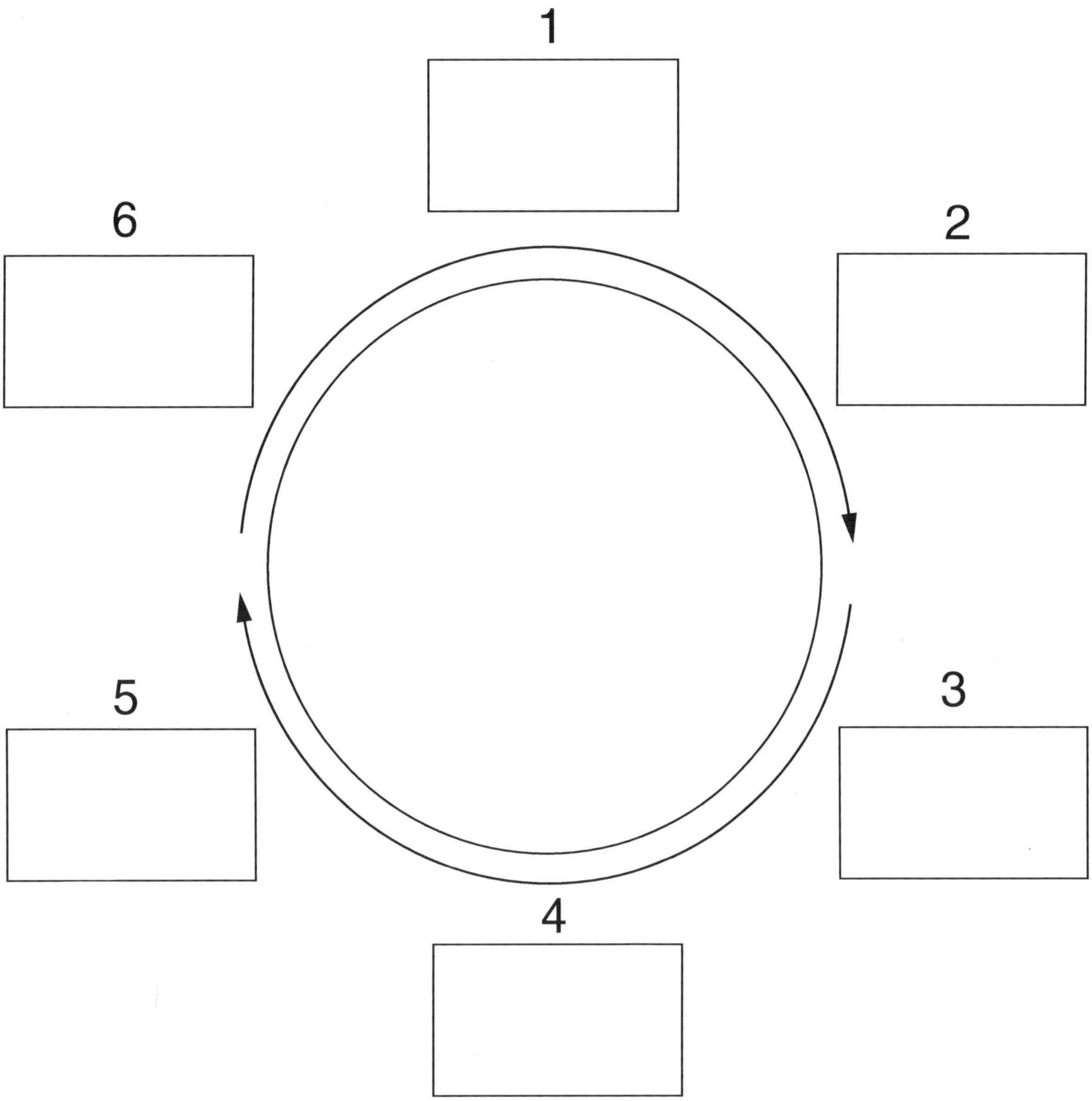

cat	**cow**	**dog**	**farmer**	**mother**	**tree**

Alice and Her Mother, p. 38

Alice was a little girl who wanted to play all day.

Her mother thought she would grow to be an idle girl if she played so much.

"You are old enough to help me, little daughter," she said one day. "Even though you are a tiny girl, you can sing little sister to sleep."

But the little girl said, "Oh, Mother, I want to play. I don't want to sing to Sister. Please let me go to the meadow. The sheep plays there all day. I want to play all day, too."

So her mother said she might play all day in the meadow.

Alice ran out of the house, across the garden, and down to the meadow, as fast as her feet could carry her. She saw a sheep there and she said to him, "Good morning, Sheep. Will you play with me? We can play all day."

"Baa, baa!" said the sheep. "I cannot play all day. I must get my dinner and make wool for Master. I cannot play all day."

Just then Alice saw a dog, and she ran to him. "Good morning, Dog," she said. "Will you play with me? We can play all day."

"Bow-wow!" said the dog. "I cannot play all day. I must look after the sheep; I cannot leave them alone."

Alice saw a cow in the meadow. She ran to the cow and said, "Good morning, Cow. Will you play with me? We can play all day."

"Moo, moo!" said the cow. "I cannot play all day. I must find my dinner. I want to find some corn. I give milk for your dinner. I cannot play all day."

The little girl walked along very slowly, for she was thinking. Soon she saw a horse and ran to it.

"Good morning, Horse," said Alice. "Will you play with me? We can play all day."

"Oh, no!" said the horse. "I cannot play all day. I give rides to boys and girls. I take milk to your mother. I cannot play all day."

The little girl said, "I will go home. No one will play with me."

On her way home Alice saw a little bird, and she said, "Good morning, Bird. Will you play with me? We can play all day."

The little bird said, "No, thank you. I must make my nest. I cannot play all day."

So Alice walked along to her home, thinking about all the animals who were too busy to play with her. She saw Spot, her cat, in the house, and she said, "Good morning, Spot. Will you play with me? We can play all day."

"No, thank you," said Spot. "I must find a mouse. My kittens must have their dinner. I cannot play all day. You must play alone."

Then Alice went to her mother and said, "Mother, I came home. I could not find any playmate. No one could play all day. I do not want to play all day, either. I will sing Sister to sleep."

Alice sang and sang, and soon little Sister was fast asleep.

—Selected

Alice and Her Mother

Preteach and review the following vocabulary: sister, Mother, meadow, master, home, and playmate. These are the comprehension questions for the student to answer orally:

Literal

1. What did Mother want Alice to do? Mother wanted Alice to sing to her sister.

Implied

2. Why did Mother let Alice go the meadow and play all day instead of making her sing to her sister? Mother probably knew there would be no playmate for all day and Alice would return to sing.

Vocabulary

3. What is a master? A master is a boss.

Implied

4. Why does the dog have to look after the sheep? The dog has to protect the sheep or keep them in their area.

Literal

5. What two jobs does the horse do? The horse has to give rides and deliver milk.

Implied

6. What is this story mainly about? The main idea of the story is that Alice found that no one can play all the time.

The phonics worksheet is teaching the long and short *a* sounds by classifying pictures under the correct phonic sound.

Answers:
Long *a*—play, day, may, playmate
Short *a*—Alice, ran, master, can, after, cat

Extended Activity

Enjoy listening to some lullabies like Alice's sister.

NAME________________________________**CLASS**__________**DATE**______

ALICE AND HER MOTHER, P. 38

Use the words from the given word bank to fill in the vowel sound chart.

Short A	Long A

WORD BANK
Alice ran day can after cat play may master playmate

LITTLE BOY BLUE, P. 46

There is no long version of this selection. Instead, read the poem orally and have the students memorize the entire poem on page 46 through 48.

Preteach and review the following vocabulary: horn, haycock (haystack), and under. The following are comprehension questions for students to answer orally.

Literal

1. What is Little Boy Blue's job? Little Boy Blue was looking after the sheep.

Implied

2. Why did he fall asleep? He fell asleep because he was tired or bored.

Literal

3. Where were the cows and the sheep supposed to be? The cows and sheep were supposed to be in the barn.

Implied

4. Why does Little Boy Blue blow his horn? He blows his horn to call the animals.

Creative

5. What will Little Boy Blue do tomorrow on his job? Accept any reasonable answer.

The phonics lesson is word building activity in which the child makes words from the endings *orn, eep,* and *ake*. After building his or her words, the child can select a few to illustrate.

Possible answers:

Horn, corn, born, morn, torn, shorn,
Sheep, sleep, jeep, peep, creep, beep, deep, keep, weep
Rake, cake, snake, bake, fake, lake, make, take

NAME________________________________CLASS__________DATE______

LITTLE BOY BLUE, P. 46

Write a letter or letters on the blanks to form new words.

___orn	___eep	___ake
___orn	___eep	___ake
___orn	___eep	___ake
___orn	___eep	___ake

Use these boxes to write three words you made and illustrate them.

LITTLE BO-PEEP, P. 49

There is no long version of this selection. Instead, read the poem orally and have the students memorize the entire poem on page 49 through 51.

Preteach and review the following vocabulary: tails and behind.

Have the student answer the following comprehension questions orally.

Literal

1. What was Little Bo-Peep's Problem? Little Bo-Peep's problem was that she had lost her sheep.

Literal

2. Who helped Little Bo-Peep with her problem? Little Boy Blue helped her.

Literal

3. Where did they find the sheep? The sheep were found in the meadow.

Implied

4. Why do you think the sheep went to the meadow? The sheep went to find better grass.

Implied

5. Why did Little Bo-Peep tell Little Boy Blue to bring his horn? They needed the horn to call the sheep.

Creative

6. How do you think Little Bo-Peep and Little Boy Blue knew each other? Accept any reasonable answers.

The phonics lesson is a review of the long *i* and short *i* sounds. Have the child find words in a magazine or newspaper to cut out and sort according to the vowel sounds. You may want to save this activity paper for the next phonics lesson.

The worksheet is a sequencing practice of retelling the story by using the key words *first, next, then,* and *finally*.

Answers

4, 1, 3, 2

Check illustrations to see if they match with the sentences.

NAME______________________________ **CLASS**__________ **DATE**_______

LITTLE BO-PEEP, p. 49

After rereading the story, number the following events in the order they happened. Illustrate the events in the correct boxes.

______ **They take the sheep to the barn.**

______ **Little Bo-Peep lost her sheep.**

______ **They find the sheep in the meadow.**

______ **Little Boy Blue helps her look for her lost sheep.**

First	**Next**
Then	**Finally**

Baa, Baa, Black Sheep, p. 52

There is no long version of this selection. Instead, read the poem orally and have the students memorize the entire poem on page 52 through 54.

Preteach and review the following vocabulary: lane, sir, dame, and coat.

Have the student answer the following comprehension questions orally.

Literal

1. How many bags of wool does Black Sheep have? Black Sheep has three bags full.

Literal

2. Who are the bags for? The bags are for the master, the dame, and the little boy who lives in the lane (accept Little Boy Blue).

Implied

3. Who is asking the Black Sheep if he has any wool? A little girl is asking the question.

Implied

4. What season of the year is it? It is winter because Little Boy Blue's mother is going to make him a coat.

Creative

5. What other things can you make with wool? Accept any reasonable answer.

The reading skill will be opposites. The parent supplies the words from the story (black, yes, little, boy, morning, and warm), and the child supplies the opposites (white, no, big, girl, night, and cool). The student can copy the word pairs on paper and illustrate. As an extension, this can be made into a little booklet.

The phonics lesson is the long *a* sound that is controlled by the final *e*. Use the provided worksheet for this lesson.

Answers:

Cane, mane, pane, cape, mate, rate

NAME______________________________CLASS__________DATE______

BAA, BAA, BLACK SHEEP, P. 52

Add an *e* to the ends of each word to form a new word with a long *a* sound.

Can + e = ______________

Man + e = ______________

Pan + e = ______________

Cap + e = ______________

Mat + e = ______________

Rat + e = ______________

THE PIG'S DINNER, P. 55

Once upon a time a little pig with a curly tail went out to take a morning walk. He thought he would go to the mud puddle, but before he got there he came to a garden that was full of pretty flowers. The garden gate was standing wide open. "Wee, wee!" said Little Pig when he saw the open gate. "Isn't this fine? I want to go into that garden. Flowers make a good dinner. Ever since I can remember, I have wanted to get into that garden." And in he went as fast as his four short legs could carry him.

When Little Pig went into the garden, he found that it was full of all kinds of flowers. There were pansies, and daisies, and violets, and honeysuckles, and all the other bright flowers that you can name. Every flower had a place of its own, too. The tulips were on both sides of the garden walk, and the hollyhocks stood up in a straight row against the garden fence. The pansies had a bed all to themselves, and the sweet peas were just beginning to climb up on the frame that the farmer had made for them.

"Woof, woof, nice place!" said Little Pig, and he put his nose down into the pansy bed and began to root up the pansies, for he thought that he would like to eat those pansies for his dinner. While he was enjoying himself there, Red Hen came down the road with her family of little chickens. Red Hen was looking for a nice rich spot where she might scratch for their dinner. When she saw the open gate she was so pleased! "Cluck, cluck, come with me into the garden," she said to her chicks. "Peep, peep, peep! Can we find worms there mother?" asked the little chickens. "Oh, yes, children. And how pretty the flowers are! There is nothing I like better than to scratch in a flower garden," said Red Hen, as she hurried in through the open gate. The chickens went with her, and soon they were all very busy scratching among the violets. How happy they all were!

Soon White Cow came down the road. She was on her way to the pond, but when she saw the open gate she decided to go into the garden at once. "Moo, moo!" she said. "How pretty the flowers are! They will make a good dinner."

Red Hen said, "Cluck, cluck, come in, White Cow!" Little Pig said, "Wee, wee, come in!" So White Cow swished her tail over her back and went into the garden. Then she began to nip the daisies from their stems.

"How many of us are here?" asked White Cow. But before any of them could count, the farmer came home. When he looked into the garden he saw White Cow, Red Hen, and Little Pig. "Oh, my pretty pansies and violets and daisies!" he cried. "Stop eating my flowers! Get out of my garden!"

"What is that man talking about?" asked the little chickens. "I suppose he wants us to go out of his garden," said Red Hen, and she ruffed her feathers as the farmer came running toward them. The hen cackled, the pig squealed, the cow mooed, and the farmer scolded. Away ran Red Hen and her chickens, and Little Pig, and White Cow—through the gate and down the road. "Good-bye, Mr. Farmer," the hen called back. "We had a good dinner!" said the pig. "We will come back soon!" said the cow. But when they went back the next day the garden gate was shut so tight that not even the smallest chicken could get inside.

—Maud Lindsay in *More Mother Stories*

The Pig's Dinner

Preteach and review the following vocabulary: pig, road, chickens, flowers, garden, red, and stop.

Have the student answer the following comprehension questions orally.

Literal

1. Which animals went into the garden? The Little Pig, Red Hen, her little chickens, and White Cow went into the garden.

Implied

2. What is the main idea of this story? The animals went into the garden because they thought the pretty flowers would make a good dinner.

Literal

3. Who made the animals leave? The farmer made the animals leave.

Implied

4. Why did the farmer want the animals to leave? They were eating his flowers and ruining his garden.

Creative

5. What do you think the animals will do now that they have left the garden? Accept any reasonable answers.

The phonics skill is the long *i* sound spelled with a *y*. Have your child find the words *by* and *my* in the story. See if your child can think of other words that end with a long *i* sound. If the vowel sound is spelled with a *y*, add this to the list.

Understanding that all stories have certain elements will help your child to better comprehend what he or she hears or reads.

All stories have these four elements: character, setting, problem, and solution. Use the given worksheet to guide your child in illustrating the four basic story elements for this story.

Answers:

Characters—Little Pig, Red Hen and her little chickens, White Cow.

Setting—the garden.

Problem—The animals are eating the farmer's flowers.

Solution—The farmer shouted at the animals and they ran away.

NAME______________________________ CLASS__________ DATE______

THE PIG'S DINNER, P. 55

In the boxes below, illustrate the characters, setting, problem, and solution from the story.

Characters	Setting
Problem	Solution

Piggy Wig's House, p. 59

One morning bright and early, Piggy Wig started out to build a home. What he wanted more than anything else was a house of his very own. So he traveled a long, long way, over the fields, and down the lanes, and past the orchards, until all at once, he came upon Jack Rabbit.

"Good morning, Piggy Wig!" said Jack Rabbit. "Where are you going?"

"I am going to the woods. I want to build a house," said Piggy Wig.

"May I go with you?" asked Jack Rabbit.

"You may go with me if you can help me build my house," said Piggy Wig. "What can you do?"

Jack Rabbit scratched his head with his left hind foot for a minute and then said, "I can cut down trees with my sharp teeth. You will need trees when you build the house, but you cannot cut them down."

"Good!" said Piggy Wig. "Come with me. I want you."

So the two went on a long, long way farther, until all at once they came across Gray Goose.

"Good morning, Piggy Wig!" said Gray Goose. "Where are you going?"

"I am going to the woods. I want to build a house," said Piggy Wig.

"May I go with you?" asked Gray Goose.

"You may go with me if you can help me build my house," said Piggy Wig. "What can you do?"

Gray Goose tucked one leg under her wing for a minute, and then she said, "Your house will have cracks in it. I can gather moss and stuff it into the cracks with my long bill. I can fill all the cracks."

"Good!" said Piggy Wig. "Come with me. I want you."

So the three went on a long long way, and all at once they came upon Red Cock.

"Good morning, Piggy Wig!" said Red Cock. "Where are you going?"

"I am going to the woods. I want to build a house," said Piggy Wig.

"May I go with you?" asked Red Cock.

"You may go with me if you can help me build my house," said Piggy Wig. "What can you do?"

Red Cock shut his eyes and thought for a minute and then said: "You will need to get up early to build your house. I can wake you up. I say 'Cock-a-doodle-doo!' every morning."

"Good!" said Piggy Wig. "Come with me. I want you."

So the four went on down the road until they came to the woods. Then Jack Rabbit cut down some little trees with his sharp teeth; Piggy Wig took the trees in his fore feet and built the house; Gray Goose filled all the cracks with moss; Red Cock said, "Cock-a-doodle-do!" early every morning, to tell them that it was time to get up. And they all lived happily together in their little house.

—Folk Tale

Piggy Wig's House

Preteach and review the following vocabulary: rabbit, woods, goose, and cracks.

Have the student answer the following comprehension questions orally.

Literal

1. What is Piggy Wig going to build? Piggy Wig is going to build a house.

Literal

2. Who offers to help Piggy Wig? Jack Rabbit, Gray Goose, and Red Cock offer to help Piggy Wig.

Implied

3. How did Jack Rabbit cut down the trees? Jack Rabbit used his teeth and chewed the trees down.

Implied

4. What time of day does Red Cock say "cock-a-doodle-doo"? Red Cock crows early in the morning to wake the animals.

Creative

5. Why did the other animals want to help Piggy Wig? The other animals wanted to help because they were Piggy Wig's friends.

The phonics skill is using the consonant cluster *cr* and the word base *ack* for word building. Have the child make five words that begin with *cr*, and five words that end with *ack*.

Use the provided characters to make puppets. Your child can color, cut, and attach the character to a stick to form the puppets. Have your child retell the story in his or her own words by using the puppets. Listen carefully to your child's version of the story to assess how well he or she understood the story.

NAME______________________________CLASS__________DATE______

PIGGY WIG'S HOUSE, P. 59

Color the characters from the story. Cut them out and attach them to a stick. You can use a craft stick, straw, etc. Use the puppets to retell the story in your own words.

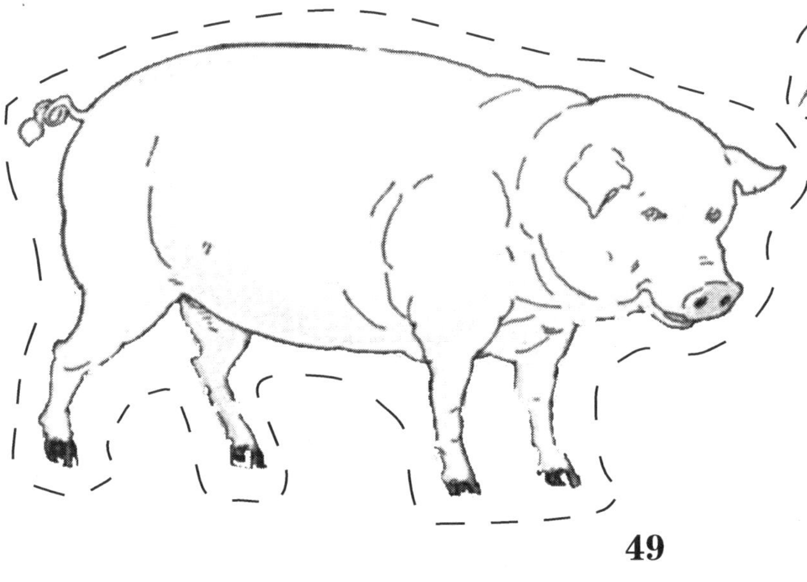

The Little Pig, p. 63

Once there was a funny, funny, little pig, who lived with his mother in a pen. One day he saw his four little feet and he said, "Wee, wee, Mother! See my four little feet! What can I do with them?"

"Wee, wee, you funny little pig! You can run with them," said his mother.

So the little pig ran round and round the pen until he was tired. Then he went to sleep.

One day the little pig found his two little eyes and he said, "Wee, wee, Mother! See my two little eyes! What can I do with them?"

"Wee, wee, you funny little pig! You can see with them," said his mother.

Then he climbed up on the trough and looked and looked all around. He saw his mother; he saw the cow; he saw the sheep.

One day the little pig found his two little ears and he said, "Wee, wee, Mother! See my two little ears! What can I do with them?"

"Wee, wee, you funny little pig! You can hear with them," she said.

Then the little pig listened and listened, and this is what he heard:

He heard the dog say, "Bow-wow!"
He heard the cat say, "Mew, mew!"
He heard the cow say, "Moo, moo!"
He heard the sheep say, "Baa, baa!"

One day the little pig found his one little nose and he said, "Wee, wee, Mother! See my one little nose! What can I do with it?"

"Wee, wee, you funny little pig! You can smell with it," she said. "Can you smell your dinner?"

The little pig was hungry and wanted his dinner, but he could not smell it. "Wee, wee, wee!" he cried.

Soon he found his one little mouth and he said, "Wee, wee, Mother! See my one little mouth! What can I do with it?"

"Wee, wee, you funny little pig! You can eat with it," she said. "You can eat your dinner."

The little pig wanted his dinner, so he hunted and hunted, but he could not find it. "Wee, wee, wee!" he cried again.

Soon a little girl in a blue dress came to the pen. She had something in a pail for Piggy. She said, "Come, Piggy! Come, Piggy, come! I have something for you. It is something good to eat."

What did the little pig hear with his two little ears?
What did the little pig see with his two little eyes?
What did the little pig do with his four little feet?
What did the little pig smell with his one little nose?
Guess what the little pig did with his one little mouth.

—Folk Tale

The Little Pig

Preteach and review the following vocabulary: pen, eyes, nose, feet, ears, mouth, and round.

Have your child answer the following comprehension questions orally.

Implied

1. Where did Mother and Little Pig live? How do you know? Mother and Little Pig lived on a farm because they were in a pen and there were other animals there that would live on a farm.

Literal

2. What did Little Pig's mother say he could do with his feet? Little Pig's mother told him he could run with his feet.

Literal

3. What did Little Pig see with his eyes? Little Pig saw his mother, the cow, and the sheep.

Implied

4. Why couldn't Little Pig smell his dinner? Little Pig couldn't smell his dinner because the girl with the food was not close enough.

Creative

5. What do you think Little Pig will do after he eats? Accept any reasonable answers.

The phonics skill is the short *e* sound. The words from the story to use as examples are *pen, hen, them,* and *smell.* Challenge your child to think of four more words that have the short *e* sound. Have your child illustrate the new words and help your child label them.

Discuss the senses, how they were used in the story and how we use them all the time. Use the given worksheet on the senses.

Answers:

Check to see that your child used reasonable answers in the blanks.

NAME______________________________ CLASS__________ DATE______

THE LITTLE PIG, P. 63

Read the following sentences. Think of words to write on the blank that make each sentence true. Use the space below each sentence to illustrate what you wrote about your senses.

I can taste ______________________ with my ______________________.

I can hear ______________________ with my ______________________.

I can see ______________________ with my ______________________.

I can smell ______________________ with my ______________________.

I can touch ______________________ with my ______________________.

Little Rabbit, p. 70

One bright day in spring, Little Rabbit went out to find some dinner. He hopped along and hopped along, until at last he came to a hillside all covered with pretty pink and white clovers. Now if there was anything in the wide, wide world that Little Rabbit liked to eat it was little pink and white clovers. So he began to run from flower to flower, eating the sweet, juicy buds as fast as he could. Just then a little girl came along and saw him. "Stop, stop, Little Rabbit!" she called out. "Where are you going? Do not run away from me." Little Rabbit jumped behind some tall white flowers and hid himself, for he had never seen a girl before and he was frightened. The girl looked all around and called out, "I cannot see you now, Little Rabbit! Where are you?" By and by Little Rabbit peeped out to watch her. He said to himself, "I wonder if that two-legged animal has come here to eat the nice juicy clovers." And he peeped out and peeped out at the little girl to see if she would get down on the ground to nibble at the flowers, just as he had been doing. At last he peeped out so far that the little girl saw where he was hiding. "Oh, now I see you, Little Rabbit!" she cried. "You are behind the flowers. You are in the pretty clovers." Then for a long time, the little girl stood looking at Little Rabbit, to see what he would do; and Little Rabbit sat looking at the little girl to see what she would do.

Little Rabbit kept saying to himself, "What a funny animal that is! It has only two legs to stand on! I don't believe it knows how to eat clovers. I will show it how to nibble the sweet, juicy buds; there are plenty here for us both." But as soon as Little Rabbit began to eat the clovers the little girl cried out, "Stop, stop, Little Rabbit! Do not eat the clovers. They are so pretty! Some are pink like your eyes and some are white like your ears. The clovers are so little now. They are just little clover children. Soon they will be big and then you may eat them!" But Little Rabbit kept on eating the clovers as fast as he could. He was such a little rabbit that he didn't know what the girl was saying to him. Just then the little girl remembered that it was her dinner time, so she walked slowly away, waving her handkerchief and calling back, "Good-bye, Little Rabbit, good-bye!" But Little Rabbit was so busy eating the little clover children that were pink like his eyes and white like his ears that he did not even hear what the little girl said.

—L. E. Oeth

Little Rabbit

Preteach and review the following vocabulary: clovers and good-bye.

The phonics skill is the *ow* sound. Practice this by finding rhyming words for *now* and *flower.* After the words are written down on paper, have the child circle the *ow* in each word as he or she reads the words back to you. Use the provided worksheet to help your child fill in the sentence transformations with words of his or her choice.

Answers:

The key is to think of something that eats for the first blank and then to think of something it should not eat for the second blank. Then think of something it can eat for the second sentence. You can fill in the blanks orally at first with different choices. Then have your child select a favorite example to write and illustrate.

NAME______________________________**CLASS**__________**DATE**______

LITTLE RABBIT, p. 70

Complete the following sentences. Illustrate each sentence in the space below it.

Stop little ____________________. Do not eat the ____________________.

Yes, little____________________. You can eat the ____________________.

Jack Rabbit's Visit, p. 72

In a hole in a big oak tree Father Squirrel had made his home. He was such a pretty fellow, with his bright eyes and his long bushy tail. He was very careful about little things and always saved up a store of nuts for the winter. He brought up his family in the same way. Mother Squirrel and three little squirrels lived with him, and they were all of them just as careful and saving as could be. There was never so much as an acorn wasted in Father Squirrel's house, and one of the very first things he and Mother Squirrel taught their children was to lay up a store of food so that they would have plenty to eat in the winter. They were nice little things, these children; they had big eyes and big tails. They played in the trees and on the ground, too, and they had no end of fun.

On this cold autumn day about which I am telling you, Father Squirrel and Mother Squirrel and the three little ones were all at home eating nuts in the old oak tree. All at once there came a tiny tap on the bark of the tree, outside the door. It was a very weak tap, so low that Mother Squirrel was not sure that anyone had knocked. She listened and soon she heard another tap—this time a little louder. Father Squirrel heard the knock, too, so he went to the door to see who was outside. He could hardly believe his eyes when he saw Jack Rabbit standing there! He had never seen a rabbit in a tree before in all his life. "Hello, Jack Rabbit!" said Father Squirrel. "How did you ever climb up this tree?" "I didn't climb up the tree," answered the rabbit. "This branch I am standing on reaches all the way from the ground to your front door, so I just walked along until I came to your house. May I come in?" "Yes, come in," said Father Squirrel. Jack Rabbit came hopping into the house. "Sit down," said Mother Squirrel. So Jack Rabbit sat down upon the floor. Then one of the little squirrels rolled some hickory nuts up to him and said, "Eat some nuts!" "No, thank you, Little Squirrel," said Jack Rabbit. "I do not like nuts."

When Jack Rabbit was warmed and rested, Mother Squirrel sent her little ones to bed. Then she and Father Squirrel had a long talk with their visitor. "Rabbit, where do you live?" asked Mother Squirrel. "I live in the ground; I have a warm hole there," answered Jack Rabbit. "What do you eat?" asked Father Squirrel. Jack Rabbit said, "Oh, I eat leaves. What do you eat, Squirrel?" Father Squirrel said, "We eat nuts and acorns. In the fall we store them away for winter. All my family helps me. So we have plenty of nuts and acorns for the winter, and enough for a friend, too, if you will just learn to eat them. Will you come to live with us?" "No," answered Jack Rabbit. "I cannot live in a tree and I could never learn to eat nuts. I must go now. Good-bye!" So away went Jack Rabbit to his nice warm hole in the ground.

—Mary Dendy

JACK RABBIT'S VISIT

Preteach and review the following vocabulary: Father, squirrel, ground, nuts, floor, and hole.

Have your child answer the following comprehension questions orally.

Literal

1. How many squirrels lived in the tree? Five squirrels lived in the tree. They were Father and Mother Squirrel and three little squirrels.

Literal

2. What did the squirrels offer Jack Rabbit to eat? The squirrels offered Jack Rabbit some nuts to eat.

Literal

3. Why did Jack Rabbit say "no thank you"? Jack Rabbit said that because he didn't like nuts.

Implied

4. What is the main idea of this story? The main idea of the story is that different animals, like people, have different ways of living.

Creative

5. If you could talk to the squirrels, what would you ask them? Accept any reasonable answers.

The phonics skill is to introduce the inflectional endings *ing* and *ed*. Explain that the *ing* ending means the event is happening now. The *ed* ending means the event has already happened. Use the provided worksheet to practice using these word endings.

Answers:

1. sleeping
2. playing
3. smelled
4. jumped
5. walking
6. eating
7. played
8. barked
9. talking
10. jumping

NAME______________________________**CLASS**__________**DATE**______

JACK RABBIT'S VISIT, p. 72

Read the sentences below. Fill in the blank with the correct ending.

1. Shhh! The baby is sleep________.
2. The children are play________ nicely.
3. Mother smell________ the pretty flowers.
4. My brother jump________ in a mud puddle.
5. We are walk________ to the farm.
6. The girl is eat________ her dinner.
7. The boys play________ until dark.
8. The dog bark________ loudly.
9. The children are talk________ to each other.
10. I like jump________ on the bed!

Bobbie Squirrel's Tail, p. 75

Bobbie Squirrel was an early riser. One bright day he got up very early, and, whisking his long gray tail over his back, he scampered down the tree where he lived and down a little brown path in the woods. Just then Jack Rabbit was coming along. Jack Rabbit's tail was little. "Look at Bobbie!" he said. "He wants us to see his big tail. How proud he is of that bushy tail of his! I am glad I don't have to carry such a long tail as that. It would be getting in my way all the time."

Brown Owl was sitting in a tree nearby. He said, "Oh, see Bobbie! He has his tail above his back. He waves it as though it were a flag!"

But Bobbie Squirrel did not pay a bit of attention to Jack Rabbit or Brown Owl. He did not care how much they laughed at his long, bushy tail. He knew that he had a great deal of work to do between sunrise and sunset, and he knew that his big tail would help him to do it.

Bobbie Squirrel ran to a nut tree, and under the tree the ground was all covered with ripe hickory nuts. Bobbie dug a big round hole in the ground near the tree. Then he swept nut after nut into the hole. Can you guess what he used for a broom? After that he covered up the nuts with leaves that he swept with his long, bushy tail, too. He will have plenty of nuts to eat next winter. When all the nuts were safely buried, it was time for Bobbie to go home, so he hurried back along the little brown path until he came to the hollow tree in which he made his home.

Guess what Bobbie found when he got home! He found nut shells on the floor! A little squirrel had stopped there to eat his dinner and had scattered nut shells all over Bobbie's green moss floor. "Oh, dear me!" said Bobbie. "This floor must be swept." So he swept the floor with his big gray tail, until the room was as clean as it could be. And as he swept with his long, bushy tail he kept saying to himself, "How glad I am that my tail is not like that little stump tail that Jack Rabbit has! I don't see how he can ever sweep his floor."

By and by night came, and the stars began to peep down upon all the trees in the woods. Bobbie Squirrel had worked so hard all day that he felt tired and sleepy, so he curled up into a furry ball.

His big gray tail, that had been so useful to him all day, made a fine soft pillow. Just before Bobbie went to sleep he said to himself, "Poor old Brown Owl! He has no pillow like mine to put that big head of his upon!"

—Carolyn S. Bailey

Bobbie Squirrel's Tail

Preteach and review the following vocabulary: brown, owl, winter, leaves, and shells.

Have your child answer the following comprehension questions orally.

Literal

1. What was special about Bobbie Squirrel's tail? Bobbie Squirrel's tail was big and bushy.

Literal

2. How did Bobbie get the nuts into the big round hole? Bobbie swept them in with his tail.

Implied

3. Why did Bobbie cover the nuts with leaves? Bobbie covered the nuts so no one would find them.

Implied

4. Why did Bobbie sweep the nut shells off the floor? Bobbie swept the nut shells off the floor so it would be clean and he would have a place to sleep.

Creative

5. In the story, Bobbie used his tail as a pillow and a broom. How else could he use his tail? Accept any reasonable answers.

The phonics skill is an introduction to the blend *sh*. Have your child brainstorm words that begin and end with this sound. For fun, you and your child can say together, "She sells seashells by the seashore."

The skill sheet is a practice for reading the color words and following directions.

NAME________________________________CLASS__________DATE______

BOBBIE SQUIRREL'S TAIL, p. 75

Read the directions. Color each animal by reading the color words and following the directions.

Color the owl brown.
Color the cat black.
Color the squirrel gray.
Color the rabbit white.
Color the bird red.

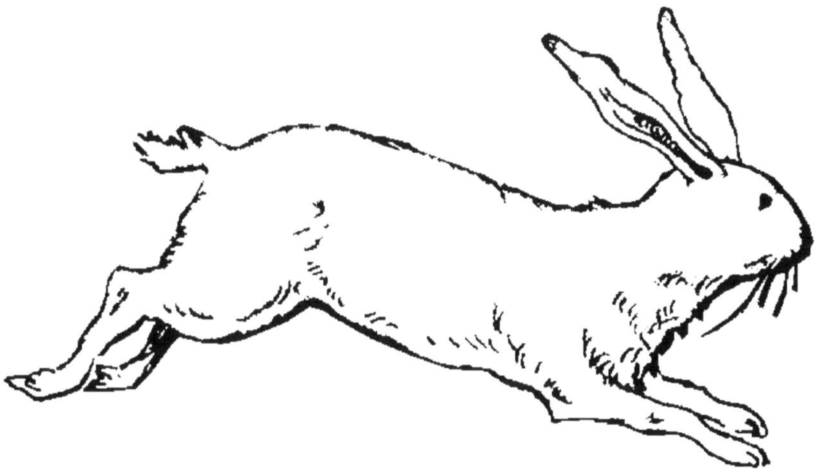

Ned Visits Grandmother, p. 78

Little Edward Wilberforce McKay was going on a journey. It seemed like a very long journey to Edward Wilberforce McKay, or little Ned, as he was generally called. The fact of the matter was that Ned was walking down the road to his grandmother's house, and he was going alone, and he had never gone alone to visit his grandmother before. He was going to show her his new red cart that his father had brought him.

Before he started out he said, "Mother, I'd like to take Grandmother something in my little red cart. What shall I take her?"

Ned's mother thought for a moment and then she said, "Perhaps she would like some cookies for her supper. Take her some of these I have just baked. Take her an apple, too."

"That will be the very thing," said Ned. So he put the apple and the cookies into his little red cart, and off he went down the road that led to Grandmother's.

Soon Ned came to a meadow by the roadside. In the meadow was a little, fat, curly-tailed pig. When the pig spied Ned and his cart and smelled the cookies and the apple, he put out his snout and ran right toward the little red cart. "Good morning, Little Pig," said Ned. Little Pig said, "Wee,wee! I want some cookies." But Ned shook his finger at him and said, "No, no, Little Pig! They are for Grandmother. Come with me to her house. She will give you some dinner." So Little Pig followed on behind Ned as he trudged along the road toward Grandmother's.

It wasn't long until they came to an old brown barn. A white hen was standing near the barn gate. She saw Ned and Little Pig coming down the road, so she got upon the gate to meet them. When they came near her, she smelled the cookies. "Good morning, White Hen!" said Ned. White Hen said, "Cluck, cluck! I want some cookies." But Ned shook his finger at her and said, "No, no, White Hen! They are for Grandmother. Come with us to her house. She will give you some dinner." So White Hen went with Ned and Little Pig as they trudged along the road to Grandmother's.

Soon they came to a house right by the side of the road. Lying on the doorstep was a little gray kitten. The gray kitten opened its eyes and saw Ned and Little Pig and White Hen coming down the road. The kitten got up from the doorstep and went out into the yard to meet them. "Good morning, Gray Kitten!" said Ned. Gray Kitten said, "Mew, mew! I want some cookies." But Ned shook his finger at him and said, "No, no, Gray Kitten! They are for Grandmother. Come with us to her house. She will give you some dinner." So Gray Kitten went with Ned and Little Pig and White Hen, as they trudged along the road to Grandmother's.

After a while they came to a big tree. A little bird, sitting in the branches, saw them as they walked along the road. Down he flew from the trees and peeped right into the little red cart. He saw the cookies there and was just thinking he would peck at them when Ned said, "Good morning, Little Bird!" Little Bird said, "Peep, peep! I want some cookies." But Ned shook his finger at him and said, "No, no, Little Bird! They are for Grandmother. Come with us to her house. She will give you some dinner." So Little Bird went with Ned and Little Pig and White Hen and Gray Kitten, as they trudged along the road to Grandmother's.

Grandmother happened to be looking out through the window. All at once she spied the queer procession coming down the road. She looked and looked. She took off her glasses and rubbed them, put them on, and looked again. "What do I see?" she said. "Oh, it is little Ned, sure as can be—bless his little heart! But what's all that coming behind him?" she said. Then she hurried out through the gate and saw coming toward her, Little Ned, and behind him the little red cart, and behind the little red cart the fat little pig, and behind the fat little pig the little white hen, and behind the little white hen the little gray kitten, and behind the little gray kitten the little fluffy bird. "Good morning, Ned! Well, did I ever, did I ever!" was all Grandmother could say, for she was so surprised. Ned said, "Good morning, Grandmother! See my little red cart? I have some cookies for you. Mother baked them just before I started out from home. I have an apple for you, too." Grandmother said, "Thank you, Ned! I like cookies and apples."

When Ned gave Grandmother the cookies and the apple, she said to him, "Now, Ned, tell me what I can give you and all your little friends." "Oh, give us some dinner, Grandmother!" said Ned. Then he told her how Little Pig and White Hen and Gray Kitten and Little Bird had wanted to eat the cookies and the apple, and how he had told them that Grandmother would give them something to eat. When he had finished, Grandmother said, "I will get you all some dinner, Ned, but first tell me what you and your little friends like." Ned said, "Little Pig and White Hen like corn; Little Bird likes bread; Gray Kitten and I like milk."

So Grandmother told them all to sit down at the big table in the dining room. Soon she brought a bowl of milk for Ned, a saucer of milk for Gray Kitten, some corn for White Hen and Little Pig, and some bread for Little Bird. They all ate and drank and had a pig-hen-kitten-bird-boy picnic in Grandmother's dining room. And when it was over, Ned kissed his grandmother and said, "Good-bye, Grandmother." And Grandmother said, "Good-bye, Ned!" and she kissed him as he started down the road with all his little friends following on behind the red cart.

As they trudged along, Ned said to Little Pig and White Hen and Gray Kitten and Little Bird, "Now you see why I would not let you eat the cookies and the apple." And they all said, "Yes, yes—we had a better dinner at your grandmother's. What a fine picnic we all had together!"

Soon they came to the big tree. "Good-bye, Little Bird," said Ned. "Peep, peep," said Little Bird. Next they came to the house. "Good-bye, Gray Kitten," said Ned. "Mew, mew!" said Gray Kitten. It wasn't long until they came to the barn. "Good-bye, White Hen!" said Ned. "Cluck, cluck!" said White Hen. Next they came to the meadow. "Good-bye, Little Pig!" said Ned. "Wee, wee!" said Little Pig. Then Ned ran home to his mother as fast as his little legs could carry him.

—Marion Wathen in *Story-Telling Time*

Ned Visits Grandmother

Preteach and review the following vocabulary: cart, yard, cookies, grandmother, ground, corn, and bread.

Have your child answer the following comprehension questions orally.

Literal

1. What did Ned take in his cart for Grandmother? Ned took cookies and a big apple in his cart.

Literal

2. What characters did Ned meet who wanted to eat the cookies? The characters Ned met were Little Pig, White Hen, Gray Kitten, and Little Bird.

Literal

3. Why did the animals go with Ned to Grandmother's house? The animals went with Ned because he said Grandmother would give them dinner.

Implied

4. How did the animals feel about Ned and Grandmother? The animals liked Ned because he was kind, and they liked Grandmother because she fed them.

Creative

5. Do you think Ned will see the animals again? Why or why not?

The phonics skill is the final *e* changing the vowel sound from a short sound to a long sound. Use the words *fat, hat, rat,* and *mat* to practice this skill. Add an *e* to the end of each word and have your child read the new words.

This story contains the compound word *grandmother*. Talk about what compound words are and practice making compound words orally. The worksheet skill is making more compound words from words given. Save the cards in an envelope or baggie to practice later.

Answers:

housework, yardwork, cornbread, daytime, nighttime, grandmother, grandfather, underground, playground, playhouse

Accept any other compound words not listed here.

NAME______________________________ CLASS__________ DATE______

NED VISITS GRANDMOTHER, p. 78

Cut out each word. Move the words around to form as many compound words as you can. Do not glue. Keep a list of your compound words.

	father	
yard	play	house
work	corn	bread
day	night	under
grand	ground	time

Little Owl, p. 88

There was once a little owl who had never been more than a few feet away from his nest. One night Mother Owl said to him, "Little Owl, it is time for you to learn to say 'Whoo, whoo!' as big owls do." But Little Owl said, "Oh, no, Mother! I don't want to say 'Whoo, whoo!'" But Mother Owl said, "You must say 'Whoo!' When boys and cats hear you and see your big eyes shining in the dark, they will be afraid and run away from you."

But Little Owl would not say "Whoo!"

"A cat will get you if you do not learn to say 'Whoo!'" said Mother Owl.

"What is a cat?" asked Little Owl.

"A cat," said Mother Owl, "has fur and four feet with sharp claws. It has big round eyes and can see in the dark. It eats mice, just as we do. But it eats little birds, too. Hide way down in your nest when you hear it call."

"What do cats say when they call?" asked Little Owl. "Do cats say 'Whoo, whoo!' Mother?"

"No, no," said Mother Owl, "cats say, 'Mew, mew!'"

"Mother! Mother!" said Little Owl, "I want to see a cat. I want to hear her say, 'Mew, mew!'"

"You are not a good little owl," said Mother Owl. "You must learn to say 'Whoo, whoo!' as I do."

"I can't," said Little Owl, and he shut his eyes tight and would not even try.

Mother Owl said, "I am going to the barn for mice, but you shall not have any for your supper."

One day Mother Owl flew away and left Little Owl sitting in the tree. "I wish I could see a cat," he said to himself. "Maybe if I say 'Mew, mew' the cat will think I am another cat and will come to see me." So he cried "Mew, mew!" over and over again. Just then a cat came through the woods and heard Little Owl, and she answered, very high and loud, "Mew, mew!" Little Owl did not hide in his nest as his mother had told him to do. He looked down from the tree, and there on the ground, near him, he saw the cat's big eyes looking up at him. When Little Owl remembered his mother had told him that cats eat little birds, he began to be frightened. But he said to himself, "The cat will not eat me; she thinks I am another cat, because I said 'Mew, mew!'"

"Who are you, up in that tree?" called out the cat. "I heard you say, 'Mew, mew!' Are you a cat?"

Little Owl did not answer. All he said was, "Mew, mew!"

Then the cat said, "You say 'Mew, mew!' but you do not look like a cat. You look like a little owl. I believe you are a little owl. Cats eat mice, Little Owl. Little Owl, can you eat a mouse?"

"Oh, yes!" said Little Owl. "I can eat a mouse."

Then the cat said, "Maybe you are a cat, after all. For you say, 'Mew, mew!' and you eat mice. But cats eat birds, too. Do you eat birds?"

Then Little Owl forgot he was pretending that he was a cat. "Oh, no!" he said. "I am a bird."

"Oho!" said the cat. "You are not a cat. You are a little owl. I eat birds. I will eat you, Little Owl!" And then that cat, with four feet and sharp claws and big round eyes, began to climb the tree.

Just then a kind little boy came to the tree. His name was Bobbie. When he saw Little Owl and the cat, he cried out, "Cat, go away! You must not eat Little Owl. I want to take him home with me and give him some dinner." Away ran the cat, and Bobbie called after her, "Good-bye, Cat, good-bye!" So Bobbie took Little Owl home with him and put him into a cage and hung the cage out on the porch.

Little Owl was not happy. He wanted to go home to his mother. Late in the night Mother Owl came and sat in a tree near the cage. Little Owl said, "Mother, Mother! I will be a good little owl. I will say 'Whoo, whoo!' I will hide in my nest when I see a cat. Take me home with you." But Mother Owl said, "No, no, Little Owl! I cannot take you with me. I cannot get you out of the cage." When morning came, she flew away.

Little Owl would not sleep. He would not eat his dinner. All day long he kept saying "Whoo, whoo!" at first very soft and low, and then very loud and high. After a while, Bobbie's mother heard Little Owl. "Bobbie," she said, "hear Little Owl! He wants to go home to his mother. Take him to his home. He will not eat, and I don't like to hear him cry."

So Bobbie took Little Owl back to the woods. "Mother Owl, Mother Owl!" he said. "Do you want Little Owl?"

Mother Owl said, "Whoo, whoo!" Little Owl said "Whoo, whoo!" too.

Then Bobbie put Little Owl in the tree where Mother Owl was sitting.

How happy they all were!

—Anne Schütze in *Little Animal Stories*

Little Owl

Preteach and review the following vocabulary: night.

Have your child answer the following comprehension questions orally.

Literal

1. Why did Mother Owl tell Little Owl he must say "whoo, whoo"? Mother Owl told Little Owl to make the sound to make the boy and cat run away from him.

Implied

2. Why did Mother Owl want the cat and the boy to stay away from Little Owl? Mother Owl was afraid the cat and the boy would hurt Little Owl.

Literal

3. What did Little Owl want to see? Little Owl wanted to see a cat.

Implied

4. Why did Bobbie take Little Owl home? Bobbie took Little Owl home to give him dinner and to protect him from the cat.

Implied

5. Why couldn't Mother Owl take Little Owl home with her the night she saw him at Bobbie's house? Little Owl was in a cage at Bobbie's house, and Mother Owl couldn't get him out.

Creative

6. If you were Mother Owl, what would you do to protect Little Owl? Accept any reasonable answers.

The phonics skill is the *ow* sound. This is the sound in out and owl. Categorize brainstormed words into two sets, one with the *ou* spelling and one with the *ow* spelling.

This is another circle story where the story begins and ends the same way. The worksheet is a circle story frame where the events of the story need to be sequenced.

Answers:

1. Mother Owl wants Little Owl to say, "Whoo, whoo," to scare away cats and boys.
2. Little Owl is curious about cats.
3. A cat came by while Mother Owl was gone.
4. Bobbie saved Little Owl from the cat by taking him home.
5. Mother Owl visits Little Owl at Bobbie's house.
6. Bobbie takes Little Owl home to say "Whoo, whoo!"

NAME______________________________CLASS__________DATE______

LITTLE OWL, P. 88

Cut out the events from the story at the bottom of the page. Sequence the events into the circle story frame.

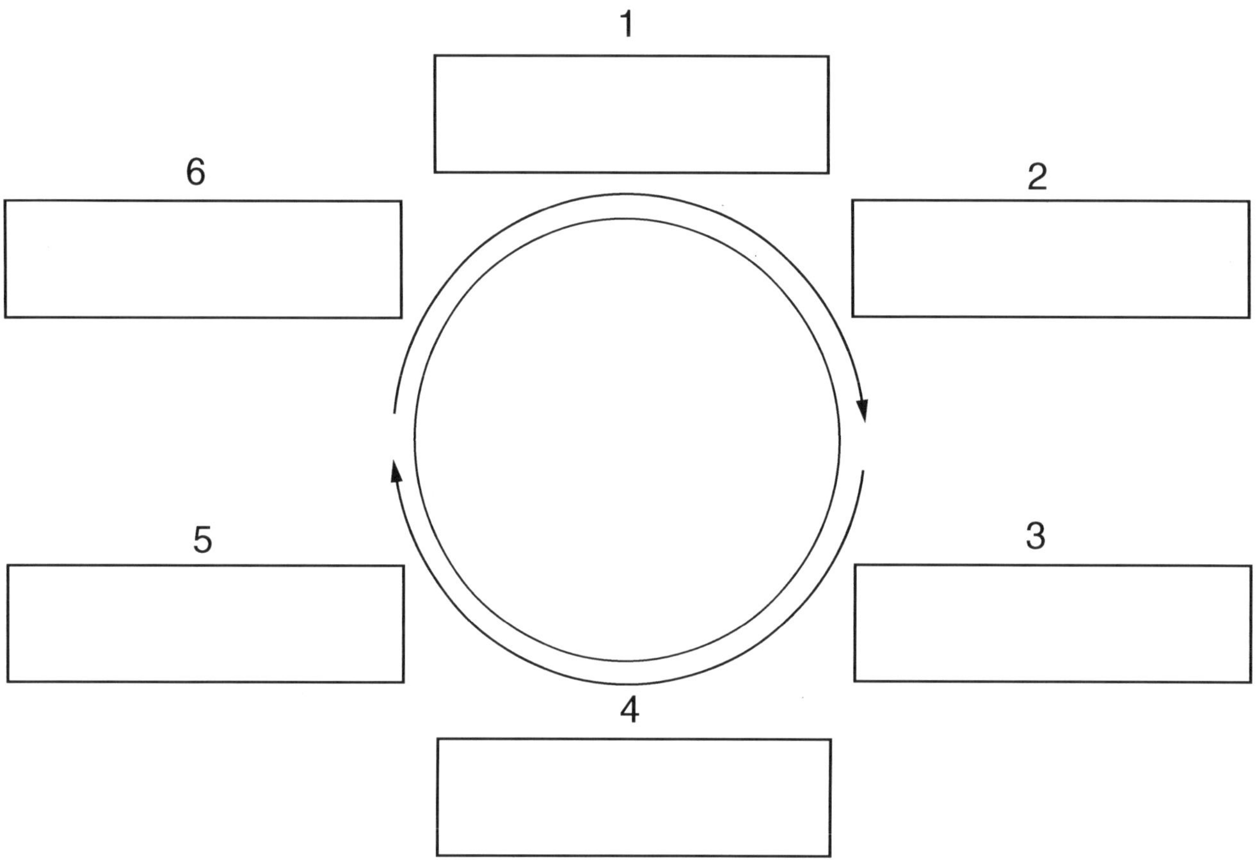

Mother Owl visits Little Owl at Bobbie's house.

A cat came by while Mother Owl was gone.

Bobbie saved Little Owl from the cat by taking him home.

Bobbie takes Little Owl home to say, "Whoo, whoo!"

Little Owl is curious about cats.

Mother Owl wants Little Owl to say, "Whoo, whoo," to scare away cats and boys.

What Brown Pussy Saw, p. 94

Two little pussies
  Came out one day,
One saw the other
  Over the way.

"Good morning, Sister,
  How do you do?"
The other answered
  With just a "mew."

One gray pussy,
  In great surprise,
Could hardly believe
  Her little eyes.

"I could never
  Stir from the bough,
That young pussy
  Is walking now."

The other pussy
  Went home with a bound;
"Mother Pussy,
  Guess what I found.

"A saucy kitten
  Sat in a tree;
Wore a brown bonnet,
  And mocked at me."
    —Kate L. Brown

What Brown Pussy Saw

Preteach and review the following vocabulary: pussy.

Note to the Teacher: The following questions pertain to the story found in the students' Reader, not to the poem on the preceding page of this guide.

Discuss the following questions with your child.

Where was Gray Pussy? Gray Pussy was in a tree.

Where was Brown Pussy? Brown Pussy was on the ground.

What did Gray Pussy say to Brown Pussy just before she ran away? Gray Pussy told Brown Pussy that she had a pretty coat.

Why did Brown Pussy run away? Brown Pussy seemed afraid of Gray Pussy.

Why can't Gray Pussy run too? Gray Pussy was part of a tree (a pussy willow) and couldn't run.

Where did Brown Pussy run when she ran away? Brown Pussy ran to her home.

What did Brown Pussy do next? Brown Pussy told her mother that she saw a gray kitten.

The skill worksheet is multiple meanings of the word *coat*. Have your child think of the different ways the word *coat* can be used. The three forms of the word *coat* that will be practiced are: an outer garment, an animal's fur, and a layer of a substance covering another.

Answers:

1. 3
2. 2
3. 3
4. 1
5. 2
6. 3
7. 1

NAME______________________________CLASS__________DATE______

WHAT BROWN PUSSY SAW, P. 94

Using the pictures that show three different definitions of coat, identify each sentence with the number that corresponds to the use of the word.

1. Coat

2. Coat

3. Coat

1. _______ Our barn will get a new coat of paint in the spring.

2. _______ The bear will grow a thick coat in the winter.

3. _______ Make sure you coat your teeth with toothpaste.

4. _______ I got a new coat and hat today.

5. _______ The dog has a black coat and short tail.

6. _______ The lollipop color will coat your lips.

7. _______ My dad put his coat on and went outside.

THE BROOK, P. 96

There is no long version of this selection. Instead, read the poem orally and have the students memorize the entire poem on page 96 through 97.

Preteach and review the following vocabulary: brook.

The phonics skill is the long *i* sound spelling *igh* as used in sight from the story. Use the worksheet to enhance this skill.

Answers

Igh—high, sigh, thigh

Ight—light, night, sight, bright, plight, right

NAME________________________________**CLASS**__________**DATE**______

THE BROOK, P. 96

Brainstorm as many words as you can that have the long *i* sound spelled with *igh* in each category. Select a few to illustrate and/or use in sentences.

igh	ight

The Windmill, p. 98

Once upon a time there was a big, tall windmill that belonged to a farmer. It had worked hard many years, filling the trough with water for the horses, cows, and sheep.

But one day it said, "I will stop! I will not go round and round. I am tired and I want to rest." So the windmill was still all day.

By and by the wind came along. It said, "Come, Windmill! Why are you not at work? I will make you go round and round."

"No, no!" said the windmill. "I don't want you to help me. I don't want to go round and round and round. I want to be still all day. I am tired and I want to rest."

The wind said, "You must go round! The horses and cows want water. I will blow for you."

The wind blew and blew, but the windmill would not go, so at last the wind went away.

All day long the windmill rested.

In the evening the tired horses came home. They had worked hard for the farmer all day in the hot sun. The cows and sheep came home, too. They were all thirsty and ran to the windmill for a drink, but there was no water in the trough.

"Oh, Windmill," they cried, "will you be kind to us and give us some water?"

Then the windmill was not happy. It was sorry there was not water. "Oh, why didn't I work today?" it said to itself. "There is no water for the horses and cows and sheep." And the windmill was so sorry that it began to creak and groan. Then it called out to the wind, "Oh, Wind, come and help me!"

The wind came at once. "I will blow for you," it said. And it blew and blew until all at once the wheel of the windmill stopped creaking and groaning and began to whirl merrily around. So the trough was full of clear, cold, sparkling water, and as the horses and cows and sheep drank, the windmill said to itself, "I will never rest again unless the trough is full."

—Kathlyn Libbey

The Windmill

Preteach and review the following vocabulary: windmill, water, drank, and help.

Have your child answer the following comprehension questions orally.

Literal

1. What was the windmill's job? The windmill's job was to go round and round and give water to the animals.

Implied

2. Why did the windmill want to be still all day? The windmill was tired of its job and it didn't feel useful.

Literal

3. What did the horses, cows, and sheep want after they came home? The animals wanted a drink of water.

Implied

4. Why was the windmill happy after he gave the animals water? The windmill was happy because he helped his friends by giving them a drink of water.

Creative

5. Tell some ways you help your friends. Accept any reasonable answers.

The phonics skill is an *ill* word building worksheet.

Answers:

Bill, dill, fill, gill, hill, Jill, kill, mill, pill, till, will, drill, frill, grill, spill, still, thrill, chill, and any other *ill* words.

NAME________________________________CLASS__________DATE______

THE WINDMILL, P. 98

This story contains words like *windmill, still,* and *will.* See how many other words you can make that have the ill ending. Illustrate two at the bottom of this page.

_____ill	_____ill	_____ill	_____ill
_____ill	_____ill	_____ill	_____ill
_____ill	_____ill	_____ill	_____ill
_____ill	_____ill	_____ill	_____ill
_____ill	_____ill	_____ill	_____ill
_____ill	_____ill	_____ill	_____ill
_____ill	_____ill	_____ill	_____ill

Who Likes North Wind?, p. 102

"Oo-oo! Oo-oo!" said North Wind to himself one day. "I am tired of playing all alone. I will go through the woods and through the towns until I find a playmate."

So he went blowing along over the fields, calling out "Oo-oo! Oo-oo! Who will be my playmate?" After a while he came to a little bird sitting in a tree. His feathers were all fluffed up, for he wanted to keep warm. "Peep, peep! Peep, peep!" said the bird when he heard North Wind. "How cold the wind is! Winter is coming. I must fly away. Good-bye!" And away he flew to hunt for a warm home in the south.

"Oo-oo! Oo-oo!" said North Wind. "I wonder why everyone leaves when I come. Nobody seems to like me. How lonesome I am! I wish I could find a playmate."

He went blowing through the woods crying, "Oo-oo! Oo-oo! Who will be my playmate?" Gray Squirrel sat on the ground, under a tree. He heard North Wind coming and said to himself, "How cold the wind is! Winter is coming. There are nuts in the woods, and I will fill my nest with them. I can eat them in the winter. My nest will keep me warm. I will go to my home in the tree." Then away ran Gray Squirrel to fill his warm nest with nuts!

"Oo-oo! Oo-oo!" said North Wind. "See Gray Squirrel run away! Nobody likes me. I am lonesome, and I wish I could find a playmate!" So he went blowing along until he came to a farmhouse. Black Kitty was in the yard. "Oo-oo! Oo-oo! Will you be my playmate?" called out North Wind. But Black Kitty did not even answer. He climbed up the doorsteps and cried out, "Mew, mew, mew! How cold the wind is! Winter is coming. I want to go into the house, for I can keep warm there. I can get some milk there, too. I can sleep on the warm floor. Mew, mew! Mew, mew! Let me come into the house!"

"Oo-oo! Oo-oo!" said North Wind. "Little Bird flew away from me. Gray Squirrel ran to his nest when he saw me coming. And now Black Kitty wants to go away from me, too. Nobody will play with me. Nobody likes me. I am so lonesome! How I wish I could find a playmate!"

Just then the door flew open and out ran a little boy named Jack. "Hurrah! Hurrah!" he cried, as he ran to the barn, waving his cap for joy. "How cold the wind is! Winter is coming, and it is going to snow.

I will make a snowman. I will ride down the hill on my sled, too. Hurrah! Hurrah! Hurrah!"

North Wind blew upon Jack's nose and cheeks until they were as red as they could be. "Oo-oo! Oo-oo!" he said. "How happy I am now! At last I have found someone who likes me! I have found a playmate! Oo-oo, Jack, oo-oo! The white snow is coming. See! It is coming now! You and I will be playmates. How happy we will be! Oo-oo, Jack, oo-oo!"

—Folk Tale

Who Likes North Wind?

Preteach and review the following vocabulary: north, cold, warm, snowman, hill, and hurrah.

Have your child answer the following comprehension questions orally.

Literal

1. How was Little Bird going to get warm? Little Bird was going to fly away to get warm.

Implied

2. Where do you think Little Bird was going to fly? Little Bird will probably fly south because most birds fly south in the winter.

Literal

3. Where did Gray Squirrel plan to keep warm? Gray Squirrel planned to stay in the nest in the tree.

Literal

4. Where did Black Kitten want to go? Black Kitten wanted to go in the house.

Implied

5. How did Jack feel about the North Wind? Jack felt excited because he ran to the barn and started to think about building a snowman and riding down the hill.

Creative

6. What would you do on a cold, snowy day? Accept any reasonable answers.

The phonics skill is the *ow* sound as in snow. Have your child find pictures with the long *o* sound in a magazine. Label the pictures and have the child circle the letters that make the long *o* vowel sound with *ow*. Group the pictures by their vowel spelling.

The worksheet is a matching activity that goes with the story.

Answers:

1. c
2. d
3. a
4. b

Name______________________________Class__________Date______

Who Likes North Wind?, p. 102

Match each character with the way it reacted to North Wind. Select a character to illustrate below.

1. Little Bird	**a. Go into the house**
2. Gray Squirrel	**b. Make a snowman.**
3. Black Kitten	**c. Fly away.**
4. Jack	**d. Go to a nest in the tree.**

How Patty Gave Thanks, p. 108

Farmer Gray always shut his animals in the warm barn at night in the fall and winter. He wanted them to be snug and comfortable for the night. But in the morning he turned them all into the barnyard. One bright November morning, when the sun was shining warmly, the gentle old cow shook the bell that was tied to her neck until it rang and rang and rang. All the other farm animals hurried to her to see why she was ringing the bell. "Good morning to you all!" she said. "I have something to tell you. Can you guess what it is?"

"Is it about a little girl?" asked Bob, the horse.

"Yes," answered the cow. "It is about a little girl. Can you guess who she is?"

Then one of the sheep spoke up and said, "Maybe it is Master's little daughter, Patty. Is it something about Patty?"

"Yes," answered the cow. "You made a good guess. It is about Patty."

"I want to hear about Patty," said Bob. "We all love Patty."

"Yes," said the sheep. "Tell us about Patty."

Then the gentle old cow began her story. She said, "What a good girl Patty is! She came to me this morning and began to stroke my forehead and said, 'Good morning, Cow. This is Thank You day. You give me milk for my breakfast. I like your good milk, so I have come to say, 'Thank you, Cow, thank you.' Then the dear child put a sweet juicy apple into my mouth and laughed to hear me crunch it. I am so glad that my milk is good and rich. I like to give milk to Patty."

"What you say is true, Friend Cow. What a kind little girl she is!" said Bob.

"Did you see Patty, Bob?" asked the sheep.

"Yes," answered Bob. "Patty came to see me, too. She said, 'You dear horse! You give me rides. Thank you, Bob, thank you!' She patted me and patted me. Then, bless her heart! She gave me a big armful of nice, sweet hay. I tell you I will give her a ride soon."

When Bob had finished speaking, the gentle old cow said, "How kind Patty is! Bob likes to give her rides; I like to give her milk."

"Did Patty thank you, Sheep?" asked Bob.

"Yes," answered one of the sheep. "She came to us, too. I can tell you I was surprised when she brought me and the rest of the flock a dish of salt this morning. She said, 'Good morning! I know what you give me, Sheep. You give me wool. The wool keeps me warm. Our balls of worsted are made of your wool, and so is the dress I have on. Thank you, Sheep, thank you!' Then she gave us some water."

When the sheep had finished speaking, the gentle old cow said, "How kind Patty is! Bob likes to give her rides; sheep like to give her wool; I like to give her milk."

By and by the cow spoke up again. "Friend Bob," she said, "did Patty thank the hens, too?"

"Yes," answered Bob. "I heard her thank them. Then she gave them some corn."

"What do the hens give Patty?" asked the sheep.

"They give her eggs," answered the cow.

Then Bob said, "Patty told the hens that she liked their eggs for breakfast, and that her mother made cake with some of the eggs, too. Patty said 'thank you' to us all. I wonder what put it into her head to come and thank us this morning."

"It was her good little heart that put it into her head to come and thank us all," said one of the sheep, wisely. "I heard Master say that this is Thanksgiving Day. I heard Patty's grandfather ask her this morning if she knew why Thanksgiving Day is kept. She answered, 'Oh, yes! It is the day to say thank you, for everything, and that is why I hurried out in the barnyard this morning.' And her grandfather said, 'To whom did you say thank you, out in the barnyard?' And Patty answered, 'Why to all of them; to Bob and the cow and the sheep and the hens!' Then I heard her grandfather say, 'I am glad that you remembered the kind, useful animals that give us so many things to make us happy and comfortable.'"

And when the sheep had finished speaking, the gentle old cow said, "How kind Patty is! Bob likes to give her rides; sheep like to give her wool; hens like to give her eggs, and I like to give her milk. Moo, moo! Good Patty."

—Emilie Poulsson in *In the Child's World*

How Patty Gave Thanks

Preteach and review the following vocabulary: girl.

Have your child answer the following comprehension questions orally.

Literal

1. Who does Patty thank? Patty thanks the animals.

Literal

2. Who gave Patty rides? Bob the horse gave Patty rides.

Implied

3. What is the main idea of this story? The main idea is Patty thanked the animals, and they felt that she was kind for remembering them.

Implied

4. Where do you think Patty lives? Patty probably lives on a farm because of all the animals around her.

Creative

5. How would you thank the animals if you were Patty? Accept any reasonable answers.

Use the worksheet for a writing and art activity about something your child is thankful for.

NAME______________________________CLASS__________DATE______

HOW PATTY GAVE THANKS, P. 108

Use the following format for writing some sentences about thankfulness. Draw a picture at the bottom to go with the sentences.

I am thankful for ____

because ____.

I show my thankfulness by

____.

The Little Christmas Tree,

p. 113

Three fir trees once lived on a hill. One tree was tall and beautiful with wide-spreading branches; one tree was not so tall, but it was growing bigger every day; one was a little tree, but it hoped that some day it would be as tall as its biggest brother.

Summer had passed, and all the maple trees and oak trees and birch trees had lost their leaves long ago. One day the snow began to come down upon the three trees, and soon it covered the ground. "Christmas is coming!" said the trees. "We want to be Christmas trees! Santa Claus will soon come and take us away. It will be great fun!"

By and by a little bird came hopping along over the snow. The little bird was lost and could not find his mother. Poor little bird! He was so cold and weak that he could not fly, but he hopped along until he came to the big fir tree. "Are you a kind tree?" he asked. "May I sit in your branches? The snow is so cold!" The big tree said, "No, no! Little Bird. I don't want birds in my branches. I am going to be a Christmas tree!" And it drew its branches away from the poor little bird.

"How cold I am," said the bird to himself. "I wish I could find a kind tree! It would keep me warm." He went on up the hill. Soon he came to the next fir tree. "Are you a kind tree?" he asked. "May I sit in your branches? The snow is so cold! I am lost, dear Tree, and I cannot find my mother." Now this tree was not kind either. It was just like the first tree. So it said, "No, Little Bird, no! I don't want birds in my branches. I am going to be a Christmas tree!"

So the little bird went on up the hill. Soon he came to the little fir tree. He was almost afraid to ask again, but he knew that night would come by and by, and that he must find a warm place to stay. So he said, very softly, "Little Tree, I am lost. May I sit in your warm branches? The snow is so cold!" Now the little fir tree was kind. It was not like the other fir trees. So it said, "Oh, yes, dear Bird! You may sit in my branches. I shall be glad to have you here."

How happy the little bird was! The little fir tree was happy, too; it stood straight up, trying its best to keep the wind off the little bird. By and by the bird heard something—he heard the sound of silvery bells. A sleigh was coming up the hill—a sleigh drawn by a reindeer! It came nearer and nearer. It did not stop at the big fir tree; it did not stop at the next fir tree; on it went until it came to the little tree, and then the reindeer stopped. "It has come to us!" said the bird.

Out jumped a man with long white whiskers. Can you guess who he was? "What a pretty tree!" he said. "I want it for a Christmas tree!" So he took the little fir tree with him in the sleigh. He took the little bird, too. "I will take you to Patty," he said to the bird. "She will keep you warm." Away they all flew over the snow in the sleigh drawn by the reindeer. How happy the little bird was! How happy the little tree was, too! For the silvery bells kept ringing and ringing—and they seemed to say, "You are going to be a Christmas tree, kind little Fir, you are going to be a Christmas tree!"

—Mary McDowell

The Little Christmas Tree

Preteach and review the following vocabulary: Christmas, three, branches, sleigh, and jumped.

Have your child answer the following comprehension questions orally.

Literal

1. What did the three trees want to be? The three trees wanted to be Christmas trees.

Literal

2. What did cold Little Bird want? Little Bird wanted to sit in the tree branches to keep warm.

Implied

3. How was the little tree different from the big tree and the not-so-big tree? The little tree was different because he was kind to Little Bird and let him sit in his branches.

Implied

4. Who was the man who took the little tree and the bird? How do you know? The man was Santa because he was in a sleigh. You could see him in the picture.

Creative

5. What will the man do with his new Christmas tree? Accept any reasonable answers.

The worksheet is a practice with number words related to Christmas.

NAME______________________________CLASS__________DATE______

THE LITTLE CHRISTMAS TREE, p. 113

Follow the directions in each box by drawing the number of items stated.

One Santa	**Two Bells**
Three Christmas Trees	**Four Presents**
Five Snowmen	**Six Stockings**
Seven Cookies	**Eight Candy Canes**

Our Flag, p. 119

(Memorize the poem.)

I know three little sisters.
You know the sisters, too,
For one is red, and one is white,
The other one is blue.

Hurrah for the three little sisters!
Hurrah for the red, white, and blue.
Hurrah! Hurrah! Hurrah! Hurrah!
Hurrah for the red, white, and blue.

I know three little sisters.
Three sisters you can tell;
For one is love, one, purity,
One, truth we love so well.

Hurrah for the three little sisters!
Hurrah for the red, white, and blue.
Hurrah! Hurrah! Hurrah! Hurrah!
Hurrah for the red, white, and blue.

—E. L. McCord

Our Flag

There are no new vocabulary words for this selection.

This would be a great opportunity to review the previous vocabulary words not mastered at this time.

Finger paint or draw a flag.

NAME________________________________CLASS__________DATE______

OUR FLAG, P. 119

Color the flag and count the stars and stripes.

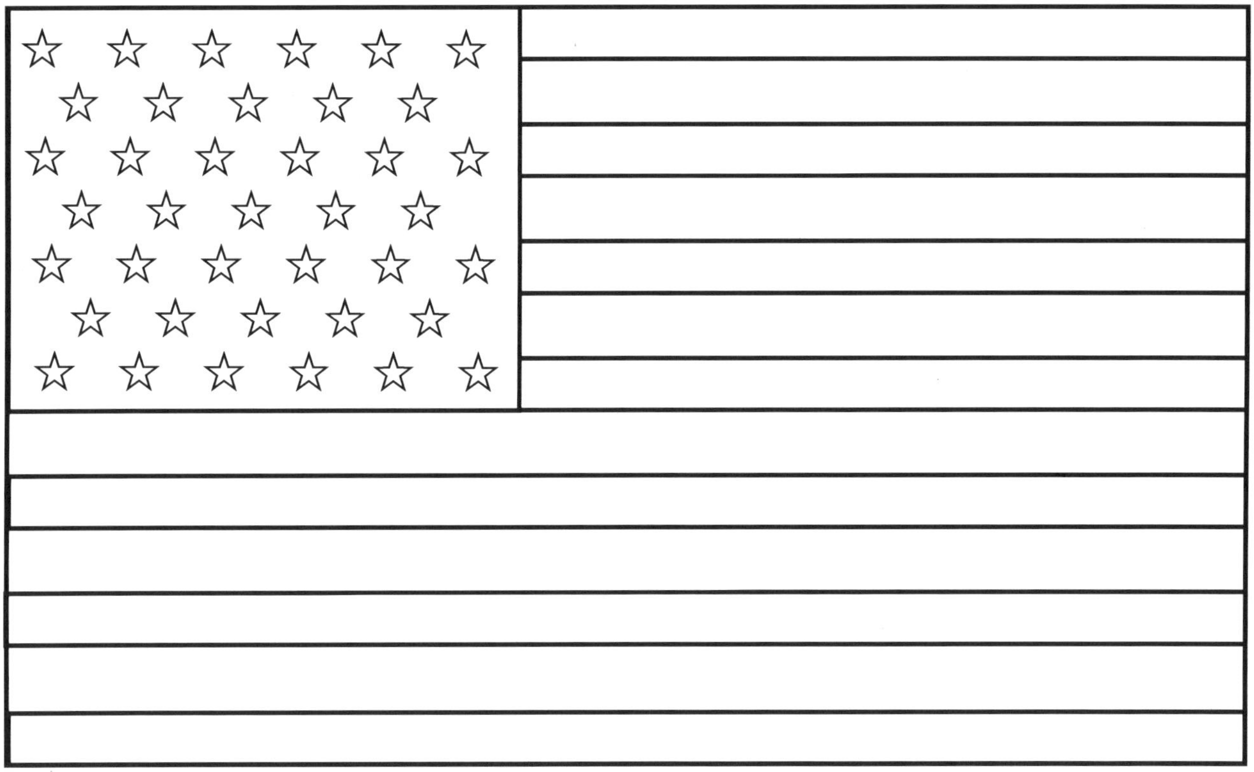

How many stars?__________

How many stripes?__________

The Easter Rabbit, p. 120

One day Little Rabbit was sitting by the roadside, when all at once he saw Ray and May coming along, hand in hand. They did not see Little Rabbit, for he was behind some bushes. "Easter is coming soon," said May. "Let us make a nest in the yard. The Easter Rabbit will see it and leave pretty eggs in it for us—blue eggs and red eggs and eggs of all colors." "All right," said Ray. "Let us make a nest. Let us begin now." And away the children ran to get grass and hay for the nest.

Little Rabbit had heard everything Ray and May said. He thought it would be great fun if he could play that he was the Easter Rabbit and put eggs into the children's nest. So he ran straight home to his mother and said, "Mother, I want to be the Easter Rabbit."

"What is the Easter Rabbit?" asked his mother in surprise, for she had never heard of such a thing in all her life.

"Oh, he is the rabbit that puts pretty eggs into children's nests every Easter," answered Little Rabbit. "Ray and May are going to make a nest in the yard. I heard them say so. I want to put eggs into it."

"Oh, no, Little Rabbit," said his mother. "Do not go away from home. You must not let Ray and May see you. They will catch you."

"I like Ray and May," said Little Rabbit. "They will not catch me." And he kept thinking what fun it would be to put Easter eggs into the children's nest.

By and by Mother Rabbit went to the garden to get some dinner, and just as soon as she was out of sight, Little Rabbit ran to see if he could find Easter eggs for the nest. Over the field and down the road he ran. Ray and May saw him and ran after him, shouting, "Stop, Little Rabbit, stop! Let us catch you. We want to give you some dinner!" But Little Rabbit ran too fast for them and called out,

"Boys and girls cannot catch me,
For I'm the Easter Rabbit, you see!"

He thought it was great fun to lead Ray and May on such a chase—but dear me, all at once he ran right into a net that someone had put in the yard! Before he could set himself free, Ray came up to him and said, "Oh, now we have you Little Rabbit! We will keep you in the barn."

So they took him to the barn and patted him and gave him green leaves for dinner. But poor Little Rabbit was frightened and wanted to see his mother. When Ray and May saw that he was not happy, they said, "Let us take him to the yard and set him free. He will put Easter eggs into the nest." So they took Little Rabbit to the yard and set him free. How he did run down the road! But as he ran away he heard Ray and May crying, and he felt so sorry for them that he stopped. "I will go back to the yard," he said. "I want to make Ray and May happy. I want to be the Easter Rabbit. I will look for Easter eggs in the yard."

So Little Rabbit ran back to the yard and hunted everywhere for pretty Easter eggs. But he could not find a single egg. Then he looked in the nest that Ray and May had made to see if any other rabbit had left Easter eggs in it. Can you guess what he saw there? He was so surprised that all he could say was, "Dear me! Dear me!" over and over. For there in the nest were two pretty little kittens—one white as snow, the other black as coal. And while he was peeping at them from behind a bush, the mother cat came along. She was carrying a gray kitten in her mouth, and she put it into the nest, too.

Just then May came to the nest to see if the Easter Rabbit had left any Easter eggs in it. When she saw the kittens she clapped her hands in surprise and joy, and called out to Ray, "Come, Ray! See what is in the nest!" Ray came running as fast as he could. "Three baby kittens!" he cried. "They are prettier than any Easter eggs." How happy Ray and May were! Little Rabbit was happy, too. "I guess I am not the Easter Rabbit, after all," he said to himself. "The cat is the Easter Rabbit!" Then he ran home to his mother.

—Anne Schütze

The Easter Rabbit

Preteach and review the following vocabulary: Easter.

Have your child answer the following comprehension questions orally.

Literal

1. What did Ray and May make in the yard for the Easter Rabbit to leave eggs in? Ray and May made a nest for the Easter Rabbit to leave eggs in.

Implied

2. Why did Ray and May keep Little Rabbit? They wanted a pet, and they thought he was the Easter Bunny.

Literal

3. How did Little Rabbit feel about staying with Ray and May? Little Rabbit was not happy, and he wanted his mother.

Literal

4. What did the children find in the nest? The children found three kittens in the nest.

Creative

5. What would you like to find in an Easter nest? Accept any reasonable answers.

The phonics lesson is a review of the long and short *e* sounds. Read the story to your child and have them identify words with a long or short *e* sound. List the words on a chart. Help your child go back and circle the letter or letters that spell the vowel sound.

Using the worksheet on story elements, have your child draw the characters, setting, problem and solution of the story.

Answers:

Characters—The characters are Ray, May, Little Rabbit, and Mother Rabbit.

Setting—The setting of the story is outside near Ray and May's house.

Problem—Little Rabbit wants to make Ray and May happy by being the Easter Rabbit and bringing eggs for the nest. Little Rabbit cannot find any eggs.

Solution—Little Rabbit finds a mother cat and three kittens and thought that the cat was the Easter Rabbit.

NAME______________________________ CLASS__________ DATE_______

THE EASTER RABBIT, P. 120

Illustrate the elements of this story.

1. Characters	**2. Setting**
3. Problem	**4. Solution**

In the Barnyard, p. 126

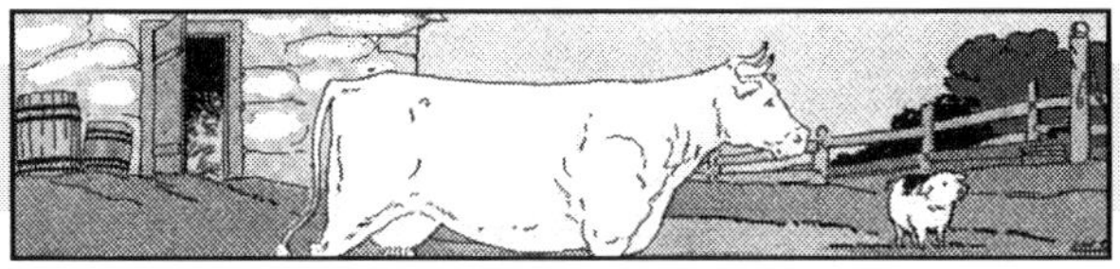

White Cow, Piggy Wig, Red Hen, and Gray Pony lived together in a big barnyard. One fine morning the barnyard folk were up very early.

"Wee, wee!" said Piggy Wig. "What a good day to eat and sleep!"

"Cluck, cluck!" said Red Hen. "What a good day to go to the garden! I can find some corn there."

"Moo, moo!" said White Cow. "What a good day to eat hay!"

"Good morning," said Gray Pony. "What a good day to give rides!"

When the other barnyard folks heard Gray Pony talk about giving rides, they all began to laugh at him.

"Wee, wee, Gray Pony!" said Piggy Wig. "I want to eat and sleep. I don't want to give rides."

"Cluck, cluck!" said Red Hen. "I want to go to the garden. I don't want to give rides."

"Moo, moo!" said White Cow. "I want to go to the meadow. Master has left haycocks there. I want to eat some of the nice sweet hay. I don't want to give rides."

But Gray Pony said, "You may spend the day as you want to, but as for me, I want to run. I want to give Master a ride."

Just then the master came to the barnyard and said, "Piggy Wig, you may eat and sleep all day. Red Hen, go to the garden and you will find something to eat there. White Cow, go to the meadow and you will find hay there. Gray Pony, come to me, and we will go to see a sick girl who lives far, far away." For Gray Pony's master was a doctor, and he wanted to make the sick girl well.

Then the master saddled Gray Pony and jumped upon his back. Away they went galloping, galloping, galloping, and by and by they came to the home of the sick girl.

The master went into the house and left Gray Pony waiting patiently at the gate. Before long the master came back to Gray Pony and said, "We helped the sick girl, and soon she can go out to play. You are a good pony. Now we can go home."

Gray Pony was so happy that he tossed his head and neighed. When the master jumped upon his back, away he went galloping back to the barnyard. He found all the other barnyard folk waiting to meet him.

"Cluck, cluck, Gray Pony! said Red Hen. "I ate corn in the garden. What a good day I have had!"

"Moo, moo!" said White Cow. "What a good day I have had! I ate hay in the meadow."

"Wee, wee!" said Piggy Wig. "What a good sleep I have had! I had a good dinner, too."

Then Gray Pony said, "How happy I am! I have had a good day, too! I helped the little girl."

—Frances Weld Danielson

In the Barnyard

Preteach and review the following vocabulary: pony, sick, and galloping.

Have your child answer the following comprehension questions orally.

Literal

1. Which animal thought it was a good day to give rides? Gray Pony thought it was a great day to give rides.

Literal

2. Where did the master go on Gray Pony? The master went to see a sick girl.

Implied

3. What did the doctor probably take with him when he left? The master probably took his doctor's bag or medicine.

Literal

4. Why was Gray Pony happy at the end of the day? Gray Pony was happy because he helped the little girl.

Creative

5. If you had a pony, where would you ride? Accept any reasonable answers.

Have your child color and cut the puppets printed on the worksheet. The puppets can be taped to a straw or tongue depressor to make them easier to handle. After the puppets are constructed, the student can act out what the animals might say or do the next day.

NAME________________________________CLASS__________DATE______

IN THE BARNYARD, P. 126

Carefully cut out the puppet characters and glue or tape to a straw or tongue depressor.

Alice and the Bird, p. 132

The bright sun was up, shining, and it was time for all children to be up, too, but a littlc girl named Alice was still lying asleep in her bed. "Wake up! Wake up!" twittered the wee little, sweet little voice of a bird just outside her window. Little Alice popped her black eyes wide open and listened. "Wake up, Little Girl! Wake up!" sang the bird. Then Little Alice hopped right out of bed and ran to the open window to look out. There sat the little bird in a tree, twittering, "Wake up, Little Girl! Wake up!"

Alice dressed herself as quickly as she could, in a neat little blue frock, and ran downstairs to breakfast. After breakfast she took her doll and went to play with Patty. At first Alice and Patty played happily with the doll and had no end of fun. But by and by the sun grew hot, and the two little girls began to grow cross. When Alice was holding the doll, Patty cried, "I want the doll! Give it to me!" Then Alice held it tight in her arms and said, "No, I want it. It is my doll!" All at once Alice heard the wee little, sweet little voice of the bird singing, "Give up! Give up!" Alice looked up and there in the tree sat the little bird, twittering, "Give up! Give up!" "I hear you, Little Bird," said Alice. "I will give up! I will give up! Patty, you may have the doll." And Alice smiled and put the doll in Patty's lap. And after that, the two little girls played happily together until it was time for dinner.

When Alice went home to dinner she could not find her mother anywhere in the house. "Oh, where is Mother?" cried the little girl. "I want my dinner!" She felt so lonesome and hungry that two big tears rolled out of her black eyes and fell on her neat little blue frock. Just then she heard a wee little, sweet little voice twittering, "Cheer up! Cheer up!" "Thank you, Little Bird," said Alice, beginning to laugh. She looked up and there sat the bird in a tree, twittering, "Cheer up, Little Girl! Cheer up!" "I will cheer up! I will be happy!" said Alice. Then she ran to play with her black kitten. She sang merrily and was happy while she waited for her mother.

By and by Alice's mother came home. After dinner she took Alice for a long ride. The happy little girl saw the blue sea and the yellow sand and the white daisy fields and the green woods. Then her mother put Alice to bed, but she was so wide awake thinking about the sea and the sand and the fields and the woods that her black eyes would not shut. All at once she heard a wee little, sweet little voice twittering, "Shut them up, Little Girl! Shut them up!" This time Alice knew without looking that it was the same little bird that had been near her all day. So she called out from her snug little bed, "I will shut them up, Little Bird! Thank you for your cheery songs!" And soon she was fast asleep. How happy the little bird was! It had helped Alice all day.

—Emily Rose Burt in *Story-Telling Time*

Alice and the Bird

Preteach and review the following vocabulary: doll and cheer.

Have your child answer the following comprehension questions orally.

Literal

1. What was the first thing the bird did to help Alice? The bird helped Alice by singing "wake up, wake up" when Alice was asleep.

Implied

2. Why did the bird tell Alice to "give up" the doll to Patty? The bird was reminding Alice to be kind to her friend.

Literal

3. Why is Alice upset when she gets home? Alice is upset because her mother is not there and she wants her dinner.

Implied

4. What is the main idea of this story? The main idea is the bird helped Alice make good decisions.

Creative

5. Tell about a good decision you have made lately. Accept any reasonable answers.

The phonics skill is using the short *u* sound. Use the following worksheet to practice the vowel sound.

Possible answers:
Up—cup, pup
Jump—bump, dump, hump, lump, pump, rump, thump, plump
Shut—but, cut, gut, hut, nut, put, rut

NAME______________________________**CLASS**__________**DATE**______

ALICE AND THE BIRD, P. 132

This story has a few short *u* words, such as up, jump and shut. Using rhyming words, add to the columns as many words as you can with the short *u* sound.

Up	Jump	Shut

Dark Pony, p. 136

Once upon a time there was a pony named Dark, who took little people to Sleepytown every night. One night as Dark Pony was galloping along the road, he was stopped by a little boy named Noddy. Noddy said,

"Take me down
To Sleepytown."

Then Noddy jumped upon Dark Pony's back and away they went galloping, galloping, galloping.

Soon they came to a little girl whose name was Niddy. Niddy said,

"Let me go, too.
Take me with you!"

Dark Pony stopped galloping, and Niddy jumped up behind Noddy. "Go, go, Dark Pony!" she said. Away they went galloping, galloping, galloping.

Soon they came to a white dog. The dog said,

"Bow-wow-wow!
Take me now!"

So Dark Pony waited while Noddy jumped down to get the dog and tucked it right under his arm. Then he jumped upon the pony's back and said, "Go, go, Dark Pony!" Away they went galloping, galloping, galloping.

Soon they came to a black cat, who cried,

"Mew, mew, mew!
Take me, too!"

When Dark Pony stopped galloping Niddy jumped down and picked up the black pussy. Then she jumped upon the pony and said, "Go, go, Dark Pony!" Away they went galloping, galloping, galloping.

By and by they came to a barn, and there on top of the barn was a red cock, crowing,

"Cock-a-doodle-doo!
Take me, too!"

When Dark Pony stopped for the red cock, Niddy said, "Come, Red Cock! You may sit behind me." So Red Cock sat behind Niddy, and away they went, galloping, galloping, galloping.

Soon they came to the woods. All at once a little gray squirrel jumped out from behind a tree and called to them merrily,

"Can you see
A place for me?"

Now Dark Pony couldn't see, but Niddy could, and she said, "Yes, Gray Squirrel, I see a place for you. Sit by the red cock."

So the squirrel jumped up and sat by the red cock, and then Niddy said, "Go, go, Dark Pony!" Away they went galloping, galloping, galloping.

What a happy company they were as they went galloping on and on, each one in his own way singing a song. Soon the songs grew soft and low, and Dark Pony began to go very slowly.

At last Dark Pony stopped, for he had come to Sleepytown. All the eyes were shut. Niddy and Noddy and White Dog and Black Cat and Red Cock and Gray Squirrel were all fast asleep.

—Folk Tale

Dark Pony

Preteach and review the following vocabulary: dark and dog.

Have your child answer the following comprehension questions orally.

Literal

1. Where did Dark Pony take boys and girls? Dark Pony took the boys and girls to Sleepytown.

Literal

2. Who do Noddy and Niddy meet on the way to Sleepytown? Noddy and Niddy meet White Dog, Black Cat, Red Cock, and Gray Squirrel.

Implied

3. Why did the characters want to go to Sleepytown? The characters wanted to go to Sleepytown so they could go to sleep.

Implied

4. Do you think this story could really happen? Why or why not? No, because animals do not talk or ride on ponies.

Creative

5. If you could ride a pony, where would you want it to take you? Why? Accept any reasonable answers.

The phonics skill is comparing the short *o* and long *o* vowel sounds. Fold a sheet of paper in half. Have your child brainstorm words with an *o* sound. The child should tell you on which half of the paper the word should be recorded.

The following worksheet reviews opposites.

Answers:

1. light
2. day
3. big
4. go
5. dry
6. cold

NAME____________________________________**CLASS**___________**DATE**________

DARK PONY, P. 136

Supply the missing opposite word from the word bank. Choose one pair of opposites to illustrate.

1. **Dark** ________________
2. **Night**________________
3. **Little**________________
4. **Stop** ________________
5. **Wet** __________________
6. **Hot** __________________

WORD BANK					
cold	**light**	**dry**	**day**	**go**	**big**

THE ALPHABET

a b c d e f g h
i j k l m n o p q r
s t u v w x y z

A B C D E F G H
I J K L M N O P Q R
S T U V W X Y Z

Word List

The following list contains the words in the *Primer* that have been developed in the *Pre-Primer** work. The number indicates the page on which the word first appears.

a, 9
and, 13
are, 15
away, 10

baa, 24
barn, 11
bird, 10
bow-wow, 33
boys, 23

can, 16
cat, 9
cluck, 26
coo, 23
cow, 23

dinner, 9
do, 29
dog, 17
dove, 29

eggs, 20

father, 16
find, 9
flew, 10
fly, 22

garden, 55
gave, 12
girls, 19
give, 23
go, 30
good-bye, 22

hen, 26
house, 12

I, 13
in, 16
is, 13
it, 10

like, 13
little, 17

may, 36
me, 13
mew, 15
milk, 12
moo, 23
mother, 20
mouse, 11

nest, 19
no, 9
not, 17

one, 14

play, 28

rabbit, 62
rained, 15
ran, 11
run, 63

said, 9
sat, 20
saw, 10
see, 14
she, 18
sheep, 24
some, 18

the, 9
them, 12
they, 15
three, 20
to, 9
tree, 19
two, 19

we, 9
wet, 15
white, 13
will 9

yes, 17
you, 16

*Lost Classics Book Company has elected not to republish *The Elson Readers, Pre-Primer.*

The following list contains the words in the *Primer* that were not taught in the *Pre-Primer* lessons. A number of these words have been developed phonetically in earlier lessons and are therefore not new to the child when read on the pages indicated. Such words are printed in italic type.

9
Alice
come

10
kittens
too

11
went

12
for

13
Spot
my
black

14
has
four
gray

15
day
was
were
sleep

16
basket
what
guess

18
her

19
pretty

20
on
from
blue

21
there
after
sang
looked

22
soon
could

23
wings
don't
wish
had
want

24
wool
keeps
warm

25
horse
rides

27
all
happy
am

28
where
Mr. *Jay*
land
of
that
far

29
Mrs.
love
how
get
above

30
Bobbie
his
apples

31
he
any
morning
have

32
who

32
tell

33
thank

34
farmer

35
with

36
bag
full

37
did
bring

38
sing
sister
meadow

39
must
make
master

40
leave
alone

41
corn
your

42
oh
take

43
home

44
their

45
playmate
fast
asleep

46
blow
horn
under
haycock

47
wake
up

49
Bo-Peep
lost
tails
behind

51
hear

52
sir
dame
lives
lane

54
coat

55
pig
down
road
came
flowers
wee

56
red
chickens
by
eat

58
stop
out
back

59
Piggy
wig
woods
cut

60
cracks
fill

61
say
Cock-a-
doodle-
doo

62
Jack
made
goose

63
once
pen

feet
round

64
found
eyes

65
ears
heard

66
nose
smell

67
mouth

68
something

70
now
clovers

71
so
be
big
then

72
squirrel
hole
ground

73
at
nuts
along
sit

floor

74
us

75
coming
Brown
owl

76
swept
covered
next
winter

77
shells
put
dear
night

78
Ned
cart
grandmother
him
cookies

81
yard

84
bread

85
ate
drank

88
whoo

91
name
kind
took

93
would

94
pussy

96
brook
both
tirili
ting

97
tumbled
sight
still

98
windmill
water

99
help

102
North
cold

104
let

105
hurrah
snow
man
hill

108
about
Patty

110
patted

111
know

113
upon
Christmas

114
branches

116
other

117
sleigh
jumped

120
Ray
Easter

123
stopped

126
pony

128
sick

129
galloping

132
bed

133
doll

134
cheer

135
shut

136
Dark
Sleepytown
Noddy

137
Niddy